*Daisy's life depends on a miracle, but she is running out of time.*

Daisy raised herself up and saw a tall man whose light jacket strained with the task of lifting the weight from her feet. Hair darkened with perspiration, face above a bandana tied over his nose, and mouth ghastly in the light, he ordered in a muffled, grunting voice, "When I lift, slide back."

Her muscles ached in sympathy when he gave a mighty tug but she jerked her bare feet upwards just in time. She winced when something sharp tore into the flesh of her leg but didn't cry out. The next moment, the stranger dropped his burden. He snatched her from the berth into his arms, flipped the blanket over her head, and started down the aisle, only to stop. "Dear God, no!"

She knew it for a prayer and tore the blanket free. A wall of flame faced them. He turned, awkward from her weight. New fire had sprung up. Daisy felt the muscles of his arms contract, then expand. "Only one way." He set her on her feet, turned toward the broken window, and groped for the blanket around her shoulders. In the light of the fire, she saw him wrap it around his hands and pound out the remaining jagged glass.

The next instant he crawled through and grunted, "Don't be afraid. There's room to stand."

Somehow she managed to climb out of the hellish scene, to breathe air a degree fresher than inside but still smoke-laden. She peered down. Fresh horror consumed her.

**COLLEEN L. REECE** is one of the most popular authors of inspirational romance. With over seventy books in print, including thirteen **Heartsong Presents** titles, Colleen's army of fans continue to grow. She loves to travel and at the same time do research for her historical romances. Colleen resides in Washington state.

### Books by Colleen L. Reece

Don't miss out on any of our super romances. Write to us at the following address for information on our newest releases and club information.

Heartsong Presents Readers' Service
P.O. Box 719
Uhrichsville, OH 44683

# Flower
# of the West

*Colleen L. Reece*

*The Flower Chronicles*

*Heartsong Presents*

A note from the Author:
*I love to hear from my readers! You may correspond with me
by writing:*

> **Colleen L. Reece**
> **Author Relations**
> **P.O. Box 719**
> **Uhrichsville, OH 44683**

**ISBN 1-55748-769-3**
**FLOWER OF THE WEST**

*Cover illustration by Kathy Arbuckle.*

PRINTED IN THE U.S.A.

*one*

Daisy Templeton O'Rourke ruefully looked at her pitch-stained hands and sprigged brown calico dress. Climbing fir trees demanded a price. Her heart-shaped, vivacious face pinkened with mischief. Daisy's eyes, that resembled clear depths in forest streams tumbling over iron-bearing rock, lighted with fun. A rebellious tendril of her coppery hair, so like her father's, held a pungent green twig that had broken in her ascent.

"God, is curiosity a sin?"

She glanced toward heaven, thankful for the early spring day's blue skies. Western Washington's capricious March weather could be showery, blustery, or downright cold. Today, however, a warmer than usual sun beamed down through the interlaced fir branches and raised Daisy's naturally cheerful spirits even higher.

"I wish they'd come," she told an inquisitive grey squirrel that scolded her behavior as improper for a young lady eighteen-and-three-quarters-years old.

She tossed her curly head.

"Don't preach, Nutley. This is 1905, not the Elizabethan Age."

Nutley, who she'd trained to eat from her hand, cocked his head and eyed her with shining eyes. She broke into laughter. He looked just like one of her Seattle school teachers who disapproved of Daisy's pranks.

The sound of footsteps sent a covering hand to her mouth. She'd be in for it if Mama and Daddy caught her perched in the tree selected solely because it sheltered a hand-hewn log bench, favorite trysting place of Daisy's parents when they did not want their daughter around.

For a moment, Daisy's conscience smote her. It really wasn't cricket to spy. Yet the need inside her to learn her fate, as she dramatically named it, prevented Daisy from shinnying down the tree and scurrying away before being detected.

Pressed against the giant tree trunk, to the further ruination of her dress, she gently parted branches enough to peer into the meadow in front of the Blarney Castle where she had been born and raised.

Mama and Daddy insisted it be called the O'Rourke Palace, but the well-screened listener wickedly preferred the name given by the loggers who helped Daddy and Uncle Harry build it twenty years before Daisy entered the family.

Now her eyes stung. It seemed strange to think of the couple walking arm in arm beneath her hiding place as old.

Heather O'Rourke moved with the same lightness of step as her daughter, despite forty years difference in age. Her brown hair, frosted with white, framed the smiling face that looked into her husband's eyes. Her hazel glance reflected the gaze that stared back from Daisy's mirror.

Daddy Brian's curly red hair held surprisingly little grey. Daisy knew from memory that neither time nor his long years at sea and even more years logging near Puget

Sound had dimmed the Irish blueness of his eyes or the accent from the Emerald Isle.

A wave of love for them both threatened to dislodge her from her perch. She quietly freed the concealing branches to their usual position, strained to hear every word of a conversation she believed would change her life forever, and put aside everything but the need to listen.

Heather's soft pink cotton afternoon dress swished when her still-gallant husband seated her. A deep sigh followed and the eavesdropper felt a pang of remorse. She hated it when Mama worried over her daughter's escapades, yet all the good intentions in the world didn't keep her from falling into mischief again. Now she sat still as a snowshoe rabbit in winter whose protective coloration offered safety from all but the keenest predator's eyes.

"Mavourneen,* what can we be fore doing concerning the colleen?"**

His rich Irish tones carried faithfully, floated upward, and betrayed a touch of amusement as well as concern.

"I only wish I knew! Just when she showed signs of becoming a young lady instead of a hoyden, along came Harry's letter. Now she's bound and determined to go to Kansas City."

"'Tis natural. She and her cousin Daphne were inseparable when they were children. Ah, how long ago it seems! Yet in other ways, I sometimes feel her blessed coming was just a little while ago."

---

*Irish for darling
**Irish for maiden

"So do I."

In the silence, Daisy reviewed her parents' life from the time Mama and Aunt Alice came West on the Asa Mercer boatload of brides. Her heart pounded. How could Mama wonder where her youngest child got her daring? Hadn't Heather Templeton fled New York and a jealous stepmother who turned her husband against Heather and her twin brother Harry? Daisy's mind thrilled to the intrepid two who had slipped away and sailed for weeks until they at last reached Seattle and found love.

"Brian, I'm afraid we haven't trained our only daughter up in the way she should go."

Heather's voice trembled and again Daisy felt guilt fall on her shoulder like a blanket. She nearly slid down the tree trunk to ask forgiveness but her father's next words stopped her.

"The Good Lord is for knowing why, if it's true," he huskily said, accent more pronounced than ever.

"Didn't we wait five long years before He sent our twins, Thomas and Thaddeus?"

A soft breeze shook the fir branches and perfumed the air with the movement of the pungent branches.

It also cooled Daisy's hot face.

"How happy we were!"

Heather instantly agreed.

"Even though we always longed for a daughter, as well. Who would have known fifteen more years would pass before God chose to answer my—our prayers?"

"I'm so glad He did," came the fervent response.

A hearty laugh destroyed the fragile moment.

"In spite of her mischief, I wouldn't trade her for all

the silks of the Orient."

"Neither would I. I can close my eyes and remember when I knew she would come."

Heather's softer laughter joined her husband's.

"The funniest thing was when we told Harry and Alice. *She* already knew she was carrying Daphne, but hadn't told us for fear of making us sad."

"A fine family Harry had," Brian said heartily. "Ephraim and Allison and Sean all married and with families of their own."

"Dear little Daphne! She was a later-in-life child, too. It seems like an eternity since we saw them off at the train station."

"All these years since he took the fine position in Kansas City, you've missed your twin, haven't you?"

"Like part of myself."

"Then why don't you take Daisy to see them, dear girl?"

At the risk of life and discovery, Daisy leaned forward and again made a peephole between branches. Her father sat with his arm around Heather; her head rested on his shoulder.

"We're for being able to afford it," Brian assured. "The mill is doing fine. The boys and I are expecting some new equipment in soon or I'd go with you."

"We've never been apart all these years," Heather protested. "I can't bear the thought of weeks without you."

The eavesdropper stuffed her fingers in her ears to shut out the private conversation. When she couldn't stand the suspense any longer, she removed them and heard her mother say, "I suppose, if you really want us to go, we can. How I long to see Harry and dear Alice. I wonder if Daphne is as timid and sweet now that she's turned nineteen?"

Envy filled the eavesdropper perched above them. Perhaps Mama wished her daughter were more like her cousin. A large wet drop sparkled in her lashes and rebellion filled her. Except for hurting Mama, what cared she how ladylike Daphne acted?

All the childhood years swept back.

She and Daphne might as well have been twins, except for temperament. Born just a few months apart, they'd never needed other girlfriends because of having each other. In fact, when her cousin went away, it took Daisy a long time to let others into her world. Although many longed to be her best friend, she refused to allow anyone to take Daphne's place.

Who among them could she tell the secret dreams and longings that kept her from being totally happy going to school in Seattle and living in the Blarney Castle. Blarney Castle was expanded from a cabin to a spacious, cool home that still faced Mount Ranier and the rising sun. Daisy's life held the freedom of forest and meadow, the color and excitement of the Indian village where native children once played.

· Thoughts of the village successfully derailed her train of thought about going to Kansas City. One of her earliest memories that stayed clear was of the tribal chief, Running Wolf. His dark face never failed to warm with welcome when Brian O'Rourke, who once risked his reputation for the chief's beautiful daughter Crying Dove, brought his own child to the village.

Sad, midnight-black eyes softened at the bright-haired child who laughed with glee when the chief presented her with trinkets: beaded moccasins more comfortable than any store shoes; pretty shells; a soft buckskin blouse and leggings she wore until they became too tight for her growing young body.

*God, why must everything change?*

First, the Indian village disbanded after the death of the chief.

Then Harry and Alice decided to move to Kansas City when offered a good job with the railroad. Busy with work and family, Harry had come for only one visit without Alice or Daphne, who was sick at the time.

Daisy remembered her uncle Harry mostly because he looked like a "man-Mama," with the same brown hair and hazel eyes and lips that curved with laughter.

Distracted by memories, Daisy's mind focused on another visit, one that left Mama in happy tears. Grandfather Templeton had come all the way from New York after his wife Adelaide died. In spite of her young years, Daisy had recognized the misery in the stooped, old man's eyes when he told his estranged daughter he had come to make peace with her.

Grandfather's voice shook and his hands trembled. "All those long years, when I longed to hear from you but was too proud to write, Adelaide kept the letters and I thought you hated me. I found them while clearing away. Can you ever forgive a self-righteous old man who thought he could run your life, nay, the world, better than the Almighty Himself?"

And Daisy found tears in her eyes from the remembered

glory in her mother's face. Grandfather Templeton had stayed several months, and now he lay beneath a friendly cottonwood, far from the place where he'd been so important. Adelaide had somehow managed to get her greedy hands on his fortune and he died leaving no inheritance except his repentance.

The third visit that stood out in Daisy's memory arose from the summer she turned sixteen. A tall pale-faced man with snow-white hair came to Blarney Castle a few days before her birthday and spent a long time with her father. Daisy later learned he had once been a minister in the church the O'Rourkes still attended.

She'd never forget the dog-like devotion in his pale eyes when he gripped Brian's hand before he left and said, "God willing, my only son will carry on the work I forsook. He's in Alaska, the last frontier!"

For a moment his face gleamed.

"Crying Dove would be proud. She became a Christian, you know, before she died birthing our son."

Sadness shadowed his pale face.

"You never remarried?" Compassion rested in Brian's blue eyes.

"I couldn't."

The simple answer impressed Daisy. But, with the heedlessness of youth, she had forgotten about Mr. Clifton shortly after he left on the long journey north to join his beloved son. He was returning to the tiny mission begun among a forgotten Indian tribe who lived tucked away in a fold of mountains far from the despoiling influence of greedy white men, where the gospel of Jesus Christ had dropped its seeds. Now, they must be cultivated, but even

Daisy, daring and courageous, shuddered at the frozen wastes and everlasting white silence she knew reigned supreme.

How long has she been wool-gathering? The climber's attention returned to the present; she felt she'd just completed a long, hard trip.

"So, will you be for going?"

"I'm still not sure," Heather admitted.

Daisy could see the crown of her smooth, gray-brown head tucked securely against her husband's strong shoulder.

A small pulse beat in the girl's white throat, modestly exposed by the little *v* below her collar. Someday, would a man fine and wonderful as Daddy cradle her in his arms—a man who loved only his Lord more than his wife? Pink stole into the rounded cheeks and a soft light to the hazel eyes. It would take someone more than the boys and young men she knew for her to permit such embraces.

"Things were so much easier when Daisy was a baby," she heard her mother say.

"The first time I held her, then looked through the window at the July day and the meadow blooming with hundreds of white, yellow-centered daisies, I knew her name."

"And a fine one it is."

The object of their discussion grimaced. She'd much rather be called Guinevere of Yolanda or Marissa. Imagine being named for a flower so common blossoms by the hundreds abounded in every conceivable spot. Even her mother's name would be better. She thought how the transplanted heather Mama carefully brought with her thrived at first at the bigger cabin in the clearing then in front of the Blarney Castle.

Heather, such a pretty name. She couldn't imagine Mama being called anything else. But Daisy! She grimaced again and felt ashamed. What difference did it make that others called her that? It was only on the outside. Inside she could be anyone she wanted: Charlotta, Adrienne, Phillipa. She frowned. Much as she hated to admit it, none of those names fit her most secret, exciting dream of the future.

Did dear Daphne remember how they solemnly vowed beneath this very tree to one day leave Seattle and carry out Daisy's dream that became her cousin's by sheer weight of persuasion? If all went well, soon she could ask her.

Another wave of rebellious wanting to break free of everything familiar and step into worlds just waiting for her arrival beat against her the way Puget Sound waves pounded the shore in storms. She set her lips in a firm line and lifted her chin. She *must* get to Daphne. Why, if she didn't, who would help carry out her dreams?

A feeling of loneliness attacked her. What if Daphne had changed? The years in Kansas City could mean her cousin no longer wanted the future they had mapped out and schemed for so long.

Daisy felt a little sick at the thought, weak because nothing had dimmed her childhood longings known only to the discreet one. Would a hundred, a thousand pictures of herself astride a faithful pony, riding across mesas, into valleys, chasing cattle down draws and beside turgid streams come to nothing? Could the long, low ranchhouse she'd built in her heart—sometimes located in Wyoming or Colorado, more often northern Arizona with its red rock mountains and pinnacles—remain a figment of her imagination?

And the strong cowboy who rescued her from one predicament after another, the just and godly defender of everything good—what about him? Even now she felt he waited until the day she came to complete his happiness.

What if she never came? *Oh, Daphne,* her heart pleaded. *Be the same. Don't have changed or everything is lost.*

A little stir below warned her the two innocent of her prying presence had risen. Dazed by the revelation that she might find her childhood companion an entirely different person, Daisy grew careless. She leaned incautiously, intending to grasp the thick end of a branch close enough to the tree trunk to support her. Off balance, her weight slipped forward.

The branch creaked ominously.

She tried to slide backwards to safety but her pitchy dress and awkward position proved her undoing.

*Crack.*

The long-suffering branch splintered, then broke. To Daisy's horror, it plummeted earthwards straight as the shaft of an arrow, its progress only slightly impeded by branches in the way. She had no choice but to hang on and ride it to the ground.

Formerly friendly and concealing branches viciously slapped her face and arms in an attempt to dislodge her.

Red welts appeared on her clear skin. She bit her lip to keep from crying out at the blows but never eased her hold.

Suddenly aware that the bucking branch which exceeded all her imaginary pitching horses had cleared the bottom row of closely growing branches and gathered speed, made heavier by its uncommon burden, Daisy continued to clutch her ungainly steed.

For one second, terror filled her.

To give standing room for visitors to the bench, the giant fir's lower branches had been cut to a good ten-foot height, leaving clear distance to the needle-covered ground. A fall on it would be painful but not disastrous, for soft earth offered a springy mat.

Daisy cried out in fear. No way in the world could she land there.

Below her stood the hand-hewn log bench, strong and menacing. It would crack her head open if she hit headfirst, the way she lay on the falling branch. She tried to twist her body but the relentless pitch held her fast.

"Please, God, help me!" she screamed.

The next moment she saw her father rudely shove Mama aside, so hard she fell. A mighty leap put him in his daughter's path. An iron grip broke her fall, yet the impact of her five-foot, six-inch, 120-pound. body hurling from above sent them both tumbling to the ground.

Daisy's face ploughed into the needles and filled her skidding nose and mouth. "Ugh!"

She spat and tried to clean her face with hands pitchy beyond redemption.

"Are you hurt?"

Heather came running, her face as white as the unconcerned clouds hovering overhead.

Still sputtering, Daisy gingerly moved arms, legs, and neck, and shook her head.

A strong hand jerked her to her feet. Never in her life had she seen her father angrier or more frightened looking.

"Daisy Templeton O'Rourke, get you to the house. You deserve a lashing."

Thunderbolts zigzagged in his voice and his blue eyes turned dark as the ocean's depths.

"I-I'm sorry," she quavered.

Shock, plus the sting of scratches, scrapes, and bruises had quelled her high spirits.

"Sorry for being caught. Go on with you."

Brian's set mouth didn't relax by the fraction of an inch.

"Heather, help with cleaning her up, will you? Not that she's for deserving your help," he added for good measure.

"It's a miracle of God she isn't lying dead at our feet."

Great cords stood out in his neck and his face grayed. His voice hurt worse than her injuries.

A few times she had heard him speak so to a recalcitrant worker but never to her. She tried to say something but a threatening flood turned speech into an incoherent mumbling and her mother drew her away, saying nothing. The reproach in the beautiful hazel eyes so like her own further wounded the hapless eavesdropper.

She stumbled to the Blarney Castle lying peaceful in the sun, torn between delayed reaction to peril, true regret for her actions, and the knowledge she had in all probability effectively scotched any chance of getting to Kansas City.

By the time Daisy had been divested of pitch, had her multitude of abrasions cleansed, and wearily fallen into bed in her pleasant room, she felt exhausted. Yet she couldn't sleep. Every time she closed her eyes, she felt herself falling again. Only in her feverish, half-conscious state, no powerful arms were beneath her. Always just before she slammed into the bench, she roused, crying, "God help me!"

A cool hand on her brow, a soft voice repeating over and over, "Don't fear. 'The eternal God is thy refuge, and underneath are the everlasting arms.'"*

A strong, but tender hand clasped hers.

Comforted at last by her father's loving hand, Daisy slept, while above her still form, Brian and Heather's glances held the same, demanding question:

*What should we do with Daisy?*

---

*Deuteronomy 33:26

# two

Dusky shadows haunted the corners of her bedroom when Daisy awakened. Her mouth felt dryer than the tiny forest creeks that had no water in summer months. She tried to sit up and groaned. Every bone and muscle in her body cried out against being forced to move. Her scratches and scrapes and bruises stung and ached. She gritted her teeth and managed to reach a sitting position, then wished she hadn't.

The mirror over her bureau reflected a face marred by ugly red welts and lingering traces of the salve Mama had applied earlier.

"My stars, I've never seen anything worse looking!"

She tore her gaze from the mirror and flopped back on the bed.

"Mama? Daddy?" It came out in a croak.

How could falling from a tree affect her voice, for pity's sake!

"We're here."

Their grave faces showed the gravity of her offense.

Heather's pallor alarmed her daughter. Brian remained unsmiling while he helped raise Daisy and propped pillows behind her back.

"May I have some water, please?"

She felt like a prisoner awaiting sentence and frankly admitted she deserved whatever punishment they meted out.

Heather brought a pitcher and glass and Daisy drank thirstily.

"Wh-what are you going to do with me?" Weren't things bad enough without her voice ch-chunking like a frog?

They seated themselves side-by-side near her bed. She remembered how all through the years they'd presented a united front. Unlike some parents who could be played off against one another, the O'Rourke family had always know it was useless to try such maneuvers.

"We haven't decided—yet."

She squirmed at the biding-our-time glint in her father's eyes, but discomfort gave way to wholehearted remorse when he quietly added, "It doesn't seem fair to deprive your mother of seeing her twin and Alice and Daphne because we cannot trust you to act as you should."

A knife in her heart couldn't have cut deeper. Daisy buried her face in her pillow and wept. Not controlled, eighteen-and-three-quarters tears, but the heartbroken sobs of a child who suddenly realizes the full results of her waywardness.

Her parents let her cry until the river of tears soaking her pillow stopped. They remained silent even when she raised her puffy face and offered the suggestion that spelled doom to all her hopes of seeing the world beyond the forests of western Washington.

"M-Mama should go. I-I'll stay here." She hiccuped and fought fresh tears.

"And what would you be for doing all day while I'm at the mill?" Brian sternly asked.

Daisy felt no more than five-years-old again. Memory of one of her most notable peccadillos flashed into her mind. The family had gone into Seattle to purchase supplies and see about schooling for the precocious youngster who could already read, thanks to Heather's training. Daisy teased to walk along the waterfront and Brian laughed, saying she must have inherited some of his love for the sea, the way she stared out over Puget Sound and measured the docked ships with her keen glance. She had lagged behind, carrying a big doll she never let out of her sight.

On their way back to the Blarney Castle, a lusty crying broke out. Brian reined in the team. Heather said, "What on earth—" and reached to uncover Daisy's doll. A black-eyed, brown-skinned papoose, face screwed up in protest, bellowed again and squirmed in the doll blanket.

"Daisy Templeton O'Rourke, where did you get this baby?"

Even now she could remember the indignation she'd felt.

"He was d'sert'd. So I brought him."

Brian whipped the team around and headed back the way they'd come.

"Saints preserve us, the mother will have the law on us."

It took a long explanation and apologies to the gesticulating squaw who had parked her child temporarily, before the O'Rourkes could convince her Daisy had't stolen the papoose. It ended with her pointing an accusing finger at the little girl and muttering dreadful sounding words in a language Daisy couldn't understand before she snatched the ragged bundle close and stormed away.

To Daisy's horror, the recollection brought a laugh.

"Young lady, I fail to find anything amusing about your willfulness."

Brians's fine lips tightened and his blue gaze bore into her.

"I-I was remembering the papoose. . ."

Her weak explanation faltered and expired. She nervously clutched her fingers until the nails made half-moon indentation in the palms of her hands.

"Daddy, Mama, I really am sorry."

"Do you think sorry is enough when it hurts others?"

She speechlessly shook her tousled head and looked down at her clenched fingers.

How many times had they played this same scene, because of what she thoughtlessly did? All her childish prayers for God to help her be a good girl; all her later efforts to control herself simply hadn't stamped out her bent for mischief.

At sixteen, local boys and young men began calling on the O'Rourkes at the slightest excuse. Daisy played pranks on some, openly scorned others, and went her merry way.

*Foolish suitors, to think one of them could win her heart. Never!*

Hurting Mama was far different. Daisy looked up, subdued for the moment.

"I could visit Thomas's wife at the big cabin during the day and come back in time to make supper," she proposed.

Brian rose and courteously helped Heather to her feet. "Your mother and I will discuss it."

He bent his piercing gaze that could sometimes be so soft and understanding directly on her.

"Since you act like a child, you must be treated as one. Stay in your room for the rest of the day."

He ushered his wife out. Neither looked back.

Rebellion shoved aside repentance. *Stay in her room!* How dare he confine an eighteen-and-three-quarters young woman? For a split second Daisy considered escaping out the window, the way she'd avoided many tedious hours of punishment over the years. She even went so far as to swing her feet to the soft woven rag rug.

Twinges of pain reminded her an afternoon in bed wouldn't be so bad. She put her feet back under the covers and pulled the blankets over her head. It did no good. Knowledge she had been completely in the wrong and had again failed to be the dutiful daughter God required her to be kept her restless.

She flung aside the patchwork quilt and surveyed the only room she'd ever had. Passing years had added comforts. The walls had been plastered and tinted the green of early spring tree buds. A white ceiling added brightness. Evidence of her parents' love showed in the white-painted bureau, bookcase, and small desk that held a vase filled with pussy willows. A few paintings of mountain and stream, valley, and the Sound warmed the room.

How she loved it!

Feeling weepy again, she turned to the One who understood.

"I knew better when I climbed the fir. Even Nutley looked shocked. I could have been terribly hurt. Please, forgive me and don't let Mama pay the price for what I did. God, thank You so much for saving me from getting smashed up."

A breeze came through the open windows, flirted with the white curtains Heather had made to complete the room, and cooled Daisy's warm face.

Gradually, she settled down and slept.

A voice roused her.

"Do you feel like getting up for supper?"

She sighed, opened her eyes, and looked into her father's face.

"Oh, yes."

It took two tries to get the stiffness from her body.

"Tell Mama I'll be there right away."

As soon as the door closed behind her, Daisy bathed her hands and face with water from the china bowl adorned with roses. The beading on the pitcher showed someone had filled it with fresh water while she slept.

"It's like You, God. Always caring for me even when I don't deserve it."

Daisy felt the parallel even more when Brian said after supper, "We've talked it over and decided Mama will go to Harry's."

He paused but his daughter didn't say a word until after he added, "You will go with her, colleen."

"I don't deserve to go." She felt she'd choke on the words.

"No, you don't." Heather said frankly. "You may as well know, Daisy, one of the reasons we decided as we did is because you haven't yet learned you simply cannot follow your own desires regardless of the consequences. I'm afraid to leave you unsupervised. You hurt others and yourself and how do you think it makes God feel?"

She didn't wait for an answer.

"I can promise you one thing. If you behave badly in Kansas City, we'll take the next train West, even if we've just arrived. I won't have Harry and Alice know how headstrong you can be."

She sighed and a brooding look came into her hazel eyes.

"Child—and you are one still, despite your age—if you continue to follow your own path, one day no one will be there to help you. Daddy and I can't live forever."

Daisy felt faint. Fear shot through her. Her still aching body tensed.

"Is one of you—ill?"

No more words came.

Heather shook her head.

"No. We just feel you need to realize no one on earth can be responsible for you except yourself."

Relief rocked her.

"I'll try. Harder than ever. I do try, sometimes."

"We know."

Heather smiled. "You just have to try harder and pray for help *before* you rush into trouble, not after. "

"I wish I were like you," Daisy burst out. "You're always so calm and never get upset except concerning me."

A quick movement of her mother's shapely hand stilled her.

Heather took a deep breath, held and released it. For the first time, she looked old to her watching daughter.

"You'll never know how hard it was for me all those years of silence between Father and me. I hated Adelaide every day until I realized how corroding bitterness ate into me and tainted everything else in my life."

Unashamed tears welled and Daisy felt she saw to the depths of her mother's heart.

"Our Heavenly Father blessed and gave me a second chance but when Father came and I learned the truth, I struggled, even though Adelaide and her meddling were gone."

"How did you get over it?" Daisy whispered.

"Shortly before Father died, we talked of her. Together we asked that our terrible resentment might be removed. Adelaide acted through greed and fear but she was not a child of God. We were."

The confession sank deep into Daisy's soul. She longed to again cry out how much she wished she could be like her mother but refrained. Yet a new determination to be more worthy came with the unpreached sermon in the nine words: *She was not a child of God. We were.*

The moment fraught with meaning passed when Heather wiped her eyes with a lace-edged handkerchief, smile, and said, "Well, if we're to go East and visit our family, we'd best begin planning what clothing we'll need and start sewing."

"I wouldn't if I were you."

The usual lights had returned to Brian's blue eyes.

"Why not? You haven't changed your mind, surely!" Dismayed, his daughter watched the mischievous smile she loved and had inherited curve his lips up.

"An Irishman change his mind? Faith, and what do you take me for? No, I'm for thinking Kansas City is a long way from Seattle. Styles may be ahead of ours. I suggest we go into the city, buy you each whatever you like for traveling and let the rest of it go. Would you like to be for shopping with Alice and Daphne?"

Daisy raced to him and threw her arms around him. "Daddy, what wonderful ideas you're for having."

Her mimicry faithfully reproduced his accent and her heart beat fast.

To purchase garments in Kansas City! She'd be the talk of Seattle when she came back decked out in the latest fashions. Daisy quickly put aside the prideful thought as unworthy, mindful of her vow to change.

☙

Yet when she boarded the eastbound train a few weeks later, Daisy couldn't help smoothing down her father's gift: a dark blue broadcloth traveling suit trimmed with soutache. She tilted her matching hat to a more comfortable angle and surveyed her mother, resplendent in navy blue and decided nothing in Kansas City could be nicer. Her new buttoned shoes shone and made up in glitter what they lacked in comfort so different from those loved Indian moccasins.

Excitement drove out everything else until the train shuddered and issued a warning whistle. Daisy looked at her father, strong and reassuring. Homesickness assailed her before the train budged. She glanced away

and lifted her gaze to the tall trees above the city and at
last to Mount Rainier.

She thought how the Indians called it the "Mountain
that was God." Even though she knew better, she still
loved the whitecapped peak visible from the Blarney
Castle except when hidden by fog or rain. She knew the
mountain's trails from hiking with her family on a few
special outings and she always felt God's hand in creat-
ing such a majestic sight. Never a day dawned without
her checking to see, "if the mountain's out." She and
Daphne had made up stories about it, shared dreams below it, and played childish games around it.

Filled to the bursting point, Daisy turned back to her
father—and knew he understood the wishbone feeling
within her. For the first time she realized how he must
have felt when he stowed aboard a ship in his boyhood
and left Ireland forever.

*Don't be a goose,* she silently ordered. *You're going
for a visit and will be back in a few weeks or months at
the most.* Yet the warm spring day felt chilly and the
glaciers on Mount Rainier forbidding, rather than
friendly.

Brian's hug warmed her; the look in his eyes reassured her.

Again the world turned rosy.

With a flutter of settling into their places and waving
handkerchiefs to the husband and father who had promised to join them if he could break free from his mill
duties, Daisy and Heather peered from the window. The
train snorted, chugged, and gathered speed until Seattle
lay behind them.

"How pretty you look," the excited girl told her mother. "That forest green is the same color as the fir I climbed."

Heather's lips that had trembled a bit at the farewell opened in a laugh.

"That's one comparison better left unsaid, my darling." Yet her eyes shone and she looked younger than at home. "I didn't know about the blue with your hazel eyes but it's perfect for your coppery hair and pink cheeks. I'm glad we each bought extra blouses. We'll change into the nicest just before we arrive."

A laugh rippled out.

"Except we have a long, long way to go before that happens."

Free of opportunity to err on the side of impropriety, Daisy stayed glued to the window. Until they crossed the Cascades and raced into strange country unlike anything she'd seen except in books, the twinges of homesickness stayed lifeless.

However, even though her eyes widened at the odd-looking brown hills and flatlands of eastern Washington, her stomach felt funny. She hadn't dreamed such barrenness existed in her own state.

Heather admitted she was as ignorant of what lay ahead as her daughter.

"My sea voyage got monotonous at times," she reminisced. "Alice and I felt we'd never come to land again and always welcomed seeing the ports we sailed into. How long ago it seems!"

"Mother."

One of Daisy's resolutions to act older was changing the familiar *Mama* to something that sounded more dignified.

"If you had it to do over, would you still run away?"

Heather stared down the long train aisle for a time before replying.

"I used to ask myself that," she said softly.

Pink streaked her cheeks.

"I felt so guilty, as if I had dishonored my father, even though it seemed I had no other choice. Yet every time I doubted, I had Brian, then the twins, and last of all you to show God's love and direction."

Daisy couldn't speak. She clasped her mother's hand and squeezed it, feeling closer than she had since she grew too big to sit on her mother's lap.

The hollowness at not having mountains around her gave way to relief when the persistent train came to the Rockies. Daisy loved every mile through their heights and depths. She did *not* love what lay on the other side.

"How can anyone live where it's so flat?" she demanded.

In her indignation, she didn't realize how loudly she had spoken or how rude her comment until Heather sent her a warning look, too late.

"Young lady, I'll have you know I'm on my way home from Oregon and glad of it," a triple-chinned woman bundled into a fur coat far too warm for the day retorted. "The whole time I visited my daughter, a circle of mountains frowned down on me, just waiting to fall and bury us alive if an earthquake came. I'll take Kansas any time, believe you me. No matter what anyone says, I don't plan to budge out of it again. Oh, I know."

She waved a pudgy hand that glittered with cheap-looking rings.

"Folks talk about the dust storms and cyclones and tornadoes. I'm telling you, that's what storm cellars are for, aren't they?"

A look of actual longing came to her face and erased some of her belligerence.

"Henry and me, we've got our storm cellar fixed up right nice and comfortable. Nothing will hurt us."

She continued, but with a dying ire. "Don't be faulting this country. For a lot of us, it's just plain home."

"I'm truly sorry," Daisy apologized, touched by her fellow traveler's defense. "I've never been out of western Washington and everything is so new."

The keen gaze softened.

"Child, the Good Lord's put beauty all around. We just need to learn to see it wherever we are."

A little smile curled above her chins.

"Oregon *was* pretty, but nothing can beat a body's home."

Daisy wholeheartedly agreed and many weary, flat mile passed by; the woman's stories of how she and her Henry came to Kansas and carved out a place for themselves kept the O'Rourkes entertained and gave them a new idea of other pioneers who had settled states far from their own.

The farther they went, the more Daisy tried to see what beauty might lie around her other than in her fellow passenger's eyes. She had to admit the Kansas sunsets beat even those over Puget Sound. Her eyes opened wide when she noticed how the sun perched on the rim of the world like a bird on a limb then fled from sight the next moment. She thrilled to a thunder and lightning storm the likes of which she'd never seen. Zigzag bolts split the ebony sky on all sides of the train until a man nearby actually read his newspaper from the flashes! Thunder pounded her ears. Torrents of rain that reminded her of Seattle descended. She didn't sleep until they ran out of the storm but the memory lingered. Her heart swelled.

*What if she hadn't come?* Never would she have known what lay outside her own tight circle of tree-lined existence.

"You have been so ladylike on our trip I find it hard sometimes to believe you're still my Daisy," Heather teased on the last morning.

She looked fresher than her daughter felt.

"It's because I'm eighteen-and-seven-eighths instead of eighteen-and-three-quarters."

She grinned and saw her mother's face light up.

"Why, before I see Daddy again I'll be a woman of nineteen, like Daphne."

"Poor old lady, nineteen-years-old and still a spinster."

Daisy laughed at the nonsense but hugged to herself the hazy picture of an unknown rider who waited for her somewhere. Her first sight of a real, live cowboy had frozen her to her seat. Silhouetted against an early sun-set backdrop on the top of a rolling foothill, the still, dark figure sent an unbelievable thrill pulsing in her body. One hand had shot up, removed the wide hat, and waved it at the passing train. The nameless man would never know the part he played in Daisy Templeton O'Rourke's life.

Instead of proving to be a disappointment, as so many

times happens when dreams become reality, sight of the lone rider astride his horse fanned the coals and embers of childhood plans and wishes into a clear, burning flame.

*Rich man, poor man, beggerman, thief, Doctor, lawyer, merchant, chief.*

The old charm of counting buttons to see who a girl would marry rang in Daisy's mind, to be quickly amend to,

*Doctor, lawyer, cowboy, chief. Who cares about any old merchant? She* planned to marry a cowboy.

"Be careful of what you ask of God; He just may be for giving it to you," Brian had told his daughter a hundred times.

Now, lost in her youthful dreams, Daisy squashed down the warning and mentally rushed ahead, faster than the speeding train carrying her away from everything familiar into a strange, inviting world.

# three

The last of the buggies drove away from the Talbot farm after rude attempts at comfort and the assurance that if "young John" needed anything, all he had to do was holler.

Only the nearest neighbor remained, a bent old man who grieved for the loss of his lifelong friend nearly as much as John mourned for his grandfather.

"Lad, what will ye do now?" A Scottish burr still clung to his speech after many years in America.

"I don't know, Uncle Dan."

John's dark brown eyes showed the strain of the past few days and his usually tanned face looked pale beneath the tossing dark brown hair disturbed by the rising wind.

"It all happened so suddenly. I took the wagon into Springfield to get spring seed, came back, and found him—gone."

For the life of him, he couldn't say dead.

"It will go hard with ye, I'm thinking."

Still bright eyes peered into John's face, then at the new mound in the pasture next to grass-covered graves with simple headstones.

"How long's it been since your ma died and ye came to live with Johnathan? Nigh onto ten year, ain't it? I remember ye weren't much more than a sprout."

"Fifteen years, actually. I'm twenty-five now."

Somber shadows from a pending storm darkened the afternoon and John's eyes.

"Never heerd tell of your pa all that time? I disremember if Johnathan ever said."

Dan shook his grizzled head.

"A few letters at first. Grandfather explained Dad was so bound up in Mother he couldn't bear the sight of the farm, or Illinois, for that matter, after she died. He headed West. Promised someday to send for me when he found treasure in the Golden West."

John's lips twisted in sympathy with the boy who'd hung onto that vow until passing years dimmed it and he had to accept Dad had vanished.

"The last letter Grandfather wrote, and it was years ago, came back marked unknown from some place in west Texas."

"D'ye think ye might look for him?"

John couldn't answer, although he knew only kindness and concern prompted the question. He moved restlessly and shivered.

"I don't know what I'll do."

"If'n ye don't mind an old man's advice, laddie, it's best not to rush into anything. Bide a wee and take time to heal. Like ye said, it's been sudden. Johnathan couldna been more hale and hearty to all appearances the night before ye came home and found him in his bed."

A film dimmed the keen glance.

"I can see him standing in the doorway waving like he always did when I turned my beasties toward hame."

The Scottish burr deepened with emotion.

"I reckon he's the best friend ever I had, barring One, the same One who'll see ye through this."

He sighed.

"Every time the Father calls another home, it makes me anxious to go and I hope 'twill be in my sleep, as 'twas with Jonathan, peaceful-like."

John nodded. Even through his shock, he'd notice the look of peace engraved on the still face, an expression of glory without a trace of fear.

"If ever any man was ready to meet his Maker—"

He broke off.

"Uncle Dan, why did God take Grandfather when he's all I had?" Anger welled. "First Mother. Then Dad. Now . . . ."

He spread his hands, palms upwards.

Calloused hands, strong and powerful as his lean, six-foot body, they showed the years of toil that had kept the Talbot place one of the finest farms near Springfield. Fertile black soil in the stretching, level Till Plains area made it the best farming area in Illinois and old Jonathan Talbot wisely developed his sprawling acres with crops that grew tall and sturdy.

"I'll be going home," Dan said.

He slowly walked to his wagon, scorning buggies, carriages, and the like in favor of his mule-drawn farm wagon.

"Mind what I told ye, lad. Trust in the Auld Book. All the fretting ye can do won't bring them back. Ye're a man now and ever since the serpent crept into the garden, man's way has been hard."

He climbed to the high seat and took up the reins. His

voice lowered, but his gaze down into John's upturned face stayed firm.

"I mind when I lost my Ainsley a few year back, life dinna seem worth living. Yet the sun kept coming up in the east, going down in the west."

He seemed to forget his companion.

"I bided a wee, kept faithful to the kirk,* and the seasons came and went."

A singularly sweet smile crossed his lined face.

"Laddie, 'twill be the same for ye."

He clucked to the mules and started toward his home.

*Could the old friend be right?* John wondered. Would time erase the day he now labled the second worst day of his life? A gust of chilled wind pierced the coat of his Sunday suit. With a final look, John unwillingly walked across the meadow, past fields black and waiting for spring planting, and entered the well-constructed farmhouse.

A feeling persisted that the nightmare would end when he stepped inside, that Grandfather would be laying the table in front of the roaring fire in the massive fireplace; tantalizing aromas from the bounteous food offerings by good friends heightened the illusion.

"My brain knows the truth but the rest of me still can't believe it," he told the quiet room.

Some of the tension left his set shoulders before its charm. Rag rugs adorned a spotless floor. A family album of pictures marched across the walls. A few live coals remained in the fireplace beneath the crane and stew contentedly simmered in the big kettle suspended

---

*Scottish for church

from it.

To John's amazement, his stomach growled in anticipation. Guilt attacked him.

How could he feel hungry at such a time? Yet hollowness demanded nourishment.

He cut the heel from a loaf of fresh yeast bread, added homemade apple jelly from a jar left on the table for him, and dished up a large bowl of stew. Grandfather's twinkling eyes and admonition through the years to, "Eat up, son," put a plow-sized lump in his throat but he swallowed and managed to down a credible supper.

*Now what?*

He wandered to the barn, hoping the necessity of chores would at least temporarily distract him. The house felt so empty without the strong man whose name he bore and who had taken on singlehandedly the task of raising a ten-year-old boy all those years ago.

No solace offered itself there. Caring neighbors had done the milking, put the milk to cool, fed the chickens and horses. Clean straw showed the stables had been mucked out.

John's eyes stung not from the pungent barn odor but from the fragrance of caring that bound men, women, and children together in unbreakable concern.

He wandered back to the house, lit kerosene lamps against the encroaching evening, and reached for his grandfather's worn Bible. He couldn't open it at first. Every evening about this time for fifteen years Grandfather had put on his spectacles, smiled over their tops, and said, "We'll be having a bit of the Book before bedtime, son." At first he'd chosen stories to intrigue a growing, restless boy—stories of daring and courage: Daniel, who refused to eat the king's meat; his three friends, who would not bow down to the pagan image; David and Jonathan.

Each time the older man mentioned them he added, "We are named for one who remained faithful to his friend, even when it meant trouble with his father. Carry your name proudly, boy. Johnathan means 'God is gracious.' Never forget it."

By his fifteenth birthday, young John knew all the Bible heroes as well as those with whom he worked, played, and worshipped. Grandfather smoothly changed course and moved on into the life of Jesus, showing His courage and daring that contrasted so sharply with Moses, Solomon, and the Old Testament prophets. He instilled into his grandson the principles that ruled his own life and came straight from the Book, along with his own broad interpretation of some things.

"God doesn't mind for us to question," he often said, to the chagrin of many a visiting preacher who found shelter and sustenance on the Talbot farm. "He gave us minds and expects us to use them. What He does mind is when we turn away and ignore Him."

The memories brought a certain measure of comfort. Right now John's questions would fill an empty barrel. He closed his eyes and let the Bible fall open, knowing whatever passage his gaze spotted couldn't help being one Grandfather had quoted at one time or another.

Yet sweat leaped to his forehead when he read the underlined scripture, *And the king was much moved, and went up to the chamber over the gate, and wept: and as* *he wept, thus he said, O my son Absalom, my son, my son Absolam! would God I had died for thee, O Absalom, my son, my son!**

King David's lament for his lost son touched John as never before. New understanding swept through him like a windstorm across a cornfield. How many times had Grandfather in his secret chambers cried out for his only son?

Even while he openly clung to Johnny Talbot's promise for the sake of his grandson, Grandfather must have privately grieved or the heavy underlining and worn-looking page wouldn't exist to betray his doubts.

John reverently closed the Bible but held it in both hands and prayed, "I don't understand but please, help me."

Not until the last spark went out in dead, gray ashes, did he put down the Book, listlessly go up the stairs to his own room, and prepare for bed, not expecting to sleep. The strain of the past few days proved stronger than will.

Hours later John awakened to Chaticleer, the rooster, crowing in the morn and demanding that the world shake off sleep and arise to the glorious sunrise painting the farm with streaks of coral and soft rose.

Somehow, John kept going. He drove himself physically so sheer fatigue brought necessary sleep. Plowing and planting, caring for the animals and farm, now his, courtesy of a straight-forward handwritten will found on top of everything else in Johnathan Talbot's bureau drawer. An attorney friend had insisted that young John find the will and bring it forward as soon as possible.

*2nd Samuel 18:33

Other than that, the bureau with its drawers of possessions stood untouched.

John gave little thought to them until Uncle Dan reminded, "I ken there'll be thing ye'll want to keep and others with no meaning, lad. When ye are able, don't fear sorting. Handling my Ainsley's things made me remember bonny times."

At last John approached the sad task. He and Grandfather had been much of a size. Much of the clothing fit and one day he'd wear it, he thought. He sighed and turned to the top bureau drawer from which he'd retrieved the will. Stacks of letters and string-tied records lay in neat piles. His delving fingers unearthed a thin bundle with familiar writing.

John set his lips. He'd know Dad's scrawl if he were in Africa. He tossed them carelessly aside, meaning to perhaps read them later. The next instant he let out a low whistle and snatched up the packet.

*What—?*

He rubbed a hand across his eyes.

*Impossible!*

Yet closer examination showed he hadn't dreamed it. The date in the blurred postmark was less than a year before. John sank to the sturdy bed next to the dresser.

What did it mean, this letter he hadn't known existed?

Like the others it had been neatly opened, so Grandfather had obviously read it.

With shaking fingers and a feeling his life would never be the same, he slid the pages from the worn envelope that mutely proclaimed how many times it had been handled.

Why had Grandfather, who scorned anything less than the truth, kept the letter's arrival secret?

> *June 4, 1904*
> *New Mexico Territory*
>
> *Dear Father,*
>    *It's finally happened. I've worked and saved enough to buy a small spread, the way I hoped. Someday, when you no longer need him, young John can come West, the way I promised—but not now.*
>    *Don't tell him about this letter. Until I'm in a position to write and send for him there's no sense getting him stirred up. Or if he's settled on the farm, maybe even married with a family, it might be best not to mention it at all.*
>    *I've never forgotten either of you. All these lonely years I've followed the tumbleweed trail; sometimes I felt ashamed to write because I'd failed miserably. Now the New Mexico sun is pouring down on me and I know you'll be glad.*
>    *I don't want to take John away as long as you need him, Father. Use your own judgment—it's always good—about when or what to tell John, even after I get the ranch and let you know.*
>                                             *Johnny*

The pages fell from nerveless hands. John Ashley Talbot's heart gave a great bound.

"Dad didn't forget." Feelings he'd been forced to ignore for years because they brought too much pain returned in full force. "Dad wants me. He's never forgotten. He said so right in the letter."

Emotion crowded the abandoned son's throat. Then more questions demanded his attention. *All these months, how could Grandfather keep from letting it slip?*

John read the letter again, this time noting how his father pleaded for secrecy until the ranch had been bought. He looked at the dates of the other letters, searching for a later missive in vain. Neither did a penciled notation show whether Grandfather had answered the last one. Excited by the find, the bewildered man continued to seek an explanation. He checked every envelope in each stack of papers—and found nothing.

Not until he dejectedly crammed his father's letter back in the envelope after a third reading did he discover what he sought. Something prevented it from going in and crumpled the edges when John tried to force them. In a fever of impatience, he ripped the envelope across and down.

A small, folded piece of paper dropped out, bearing Grandfather's writing. Almost afraid to read what it said, John opened it.

> *Dear John,*
> *You won't find this until I'm gone. If*
> *your father writes again by then, perhaps*
> *this will be meaningless. I know you will*

*wonder why I kept my own counsel when
there's naught we didn't share.*

*Son, I've had a warning. My ticker isn't
what it should be. Perhaps it's selfish, but
I want to keep you as long as I can. I need
you. I might gain a little time if I sat in a
rocker but that's not living, so I'm going
on as we have until now.*

*Neither will I burden you; it will be no
sadder when I go and so I'll keep from
prolonging the pain that comes with
knowing.*

*I hate to leave you, yet one day you'll
be coming, as well, to be with your
mother, grandmother, and me.*

*Don't let sentiment hold you on the
farm. I want you to go find Johnny, I'd
like that. Dan can help you decide
whether to sell or lease, if this be your
choice. No man could have had a better
namesake. I leave you in hands even
better than mine, the same that have
uplifted me all my life.*

The letter bore the simple signature: *Your Grandfather.*

Stunned by the revelations in the two letters, John
sprang from the room, raced down the stairs, and hurried out the door.

He hurried to the mounded dirt already sinking and
covered with new grass and threw himself on the earth

as he had done in childhood when life became sad and dreams burst like the soap bubbles in the air.

A long time later, he rose, saddled a horse, and rode off to tell Uncle Dan what he'd learned.

The old Scotsman didn't let him down.

"Weel, but that's good news!" He peered at the letters. "Ye found no more?"

"No, and I searched thoroughly." John shook his dark head and his matching eyes glowed. "It sounds like he wants me to find Dad, doesn't it?"

Dan turned cautious. His canny way of viewing life allowed for no aimless rushing around.

"Laddie, ye need to take time," he warned. "Ye don't know but what Johnny's moved on."

John's spirits fell to ground level.

"I never thought of that."

"Write a wee letter," Dan suggested. "Send it to the place this one came from."

He tapped the soiled envelope with a long, bony finger.

"I will."

The fervent agreement brought a smile to the Scot's lips and dour face, although he just nodded.

"'Tis best."

John remembered the words while he struggled with his letter.

How did a twenty-five-year-old man write to an absent father who might well still think of his son as ten-years-old? He littered the floor of the living room with crumpled pages before settling on a simple message that told how he'd found the two letters after Grandfather's death.

He closed by saying, "Do you still want me to come? I can lease or sell the farm."

Should he sign it *love*?

John shook his head and substituted, *Your son John*, feeling he'd fought a long battle to get even this close to his father.

After the letter started west, John found himself dredging up every memory of Johnny Talbot he could. A few pictures helped bring back the tall, slim man whose build his son had inherited, along with his dark brown hair and eyes. Yet there the resemblance between them ended. All the pictures and most of the memories showed Johnny's white teeth in a laughing face. John's smile came from his mother. It began with crinkles at the corners of his eyes and slowly crept over his serious face until his lips moved.

"Fifteen years won't have changed him as much as it has me," he told Dan, who had become philosopher, friend, and guide more than ever. "Why, he probably won't even know me when I find him. A ten-year-old, scrawny kid isn't much like a full-grown farmer."

"Depending on what kine of life he's led, ye'll find changes, no doot," Dan quietly reminded.

"I know. But he will still be Dad, no matter what."

A little tingle ran through him and he felt he'd just taken a solemn oath, one to be fulfilled no matter what it cost. The more he and Dan talked, and later when John went to the attorney who had recorded the will, the more he heeded their well-thought-out advice.

Selling the productive farm meant more money than

John ever dreamed he'd have. On the other hand money could run out. After consideration and a lot of prayer, he decided to lease the farm for a year. If things didn't work out, he had an anchor, a place to come back to where folks cared about him.

"I just hope I can find a good family," he told Dan the day after he made the final decision not to sell. Summer lay hot and promised a bumper crop. "In a way, I feel I should stay long enough for the harvest but that would mean not getting started until fall. There's this kind of urgency in me, a little something that prods and says to get away as soon as I can."

He shrugged, feeling foolish.

"Sounds silly, doesn't it, going after a father who hasn't even answered my letter."

"Nay. I'd not scorn the wee voice." The old man's eyes gleamed. "Ye're sure ye want to lease?"

"Yes. Why?"

"'Twouldn't have done to speak sooner but now that ye've decided, it may be the Father's providing. My nephew who left the land to try for a bit of luck in the city's tired of it and wants a place to bide. He's a good worker and would care for the farm kindly. His wife's heartsick to leave the city. If my house were bigger, I'd have them and the bairns with me; five of them there are."

"That's wonderful." John grasped the other's gnarled, strong hand. "They'll be close, too, so you won't be lonely with me gone. And Grandfather."

"Aye, but I know I'll be missing ye both," he signed.

Within a few days, signed papers and the transfer of

money told anyone interested that the new farmers would lease the Talbot place for one year. Further clauses specified the lease could be extended, should both parties agree when the time came.

John agreed to leave all the furniture and livestock; only his and a few of Grandfather's most cherished possessions went by wagon to Dan's cottage for safekeeping.

At times the young man walked the rich fields wondering if he were mad to leave the only life he had ever known. Yet the dream of finding his father pushed him on and the day came when he rode into Springfield, plunked down the right amount of cash, and went home carrying railway tickets to New Mexico.

At times the whole thing seemed dreamlike, a phantasm to be banished by the light of day. The illusion fled the moment John stepped aboard the train, bid good-bye to Dan and a few others who had come to the station, and watched the station become a speck in the distance, knowing thousands of miles stretched between this bittersweet moment and the time he returned—if ever.

# four

Daphne Templeton at nineteen little resembled the berry-stained, grubby child who once followed her cousin Daisy in and out of trouble. The rebellious flaxen curls, formerly such a nuisance in Washington State, now lay tamed and shining in the light from the sparkling chandelier with its crystal pendants that required frequent washing. The hint of mischief that still lived in her soft blue eyes only occasionally bubbled over. Once-scratched hands lay soft and white in the lap of her frilly blue gown. Modest in the extreme, her appearance reflected Daphne's personality. Not a sweeter or more Christian young woman graced the Kansas City circle of maidens, and more than one young swain hovered near her door.

Tonight Daphne's thoughts ran far afield from the would- be suitors but oh, so close to home! Father had brought to dinner the pleasant young clerk from his office. Theodore Radcliffe had sandy, well-brushed hair and eyes a shade lighter than Daphne's. From the first time she saw him while visiting Harry's place of business, Daphne found herself strangely drawn to the quiet young man whom she suspected was as reticent as herself. Or perhaps her position as his superior's daughter intimidated him. On the few occasions when he came to the tasteful Templeton home, Theodore smiled at her but didn't talk much. She rather liked him for it and found him restful compared with the brash young men who called on her. She discovered they liked many of the same things: good music; the works of Dickens, especially the unforgettable *A Tale of Two Cities.*

If the glittering damask tablecloth, crystal, and silver always used for the company—be it banker or clerk—overwhelmed Theodore, it didn't show. He had impeccable manners and never forgot to praise the cook's delicious and intricate offerings. Daphne also liked his deference to her parents. In the year since the young man began working for Father, he never lost his respectful attention when Harry or Alice spoke.

She looked at them, a little gray around the edges but filled with life and joy. A wellspring of gladness filled her. How pretty Mother looked in her soft pink dress and lace collar. Time had given her sweet face, so like her daughter's, laugh wrinkles that actually enhanced rather than detracted from her attractiveness. Father looked like a mischievous boy who just hadn't discovered how many years had passed since he ran away from home to seek fame and fortune in the West. The look in his hazel eyes when he glanced at Alice showed he viewed her as even more beautiful and charming than the day she stepped off the ship in Seattle and into his waiting arms.

Daphne stifled a sigh and quite unconsciously turned toward Theodore. For a moment she fancied she saw a similar look in the blue gaze fixed on her. It set her heart fluttering beneath the delicate bodice of her dress but vanished so quickly she couldn't be sure she'd really seen it.

"Well, daughter, it won't be long until Heather and Daisy arrive." Harry's face glowed at the thought of his twin's coming. "I wonder if your cousin and playmate has grown up to be as fine a woman as you." He laughed when a rich blush rose from the slightly rounded neck of her dress and spread over her fair skin. "Not that I expect it." He turned to Theodore. "If ever a child could fall into mischief, Daisy O'Rourke's that one. She inherited her mother's grace but her father's red hair and spirit." He broke off to laugh again.

"Wait until you hear the latest. Heather couldn't help telling me that—"

"Father, are you being quite fair to Daisy?" her loyal defender interrupted. "Telling tales out of school isn't really cricket."

Harry's eyes opened wide. "Why, you know she wouldn't care. After all, it's just family—and Theodore, of course," he belatedly added. "My word, if I'm not beginning to feel you're one of us, lad." He smiled down the table at the embarrassed clerk.

Mercy, couldn't he see how flustered Theodore had grown, Daphne wondered. She quickly said, "Oh, go ahead and tell us" and found her reward in the grateful glance she received from their visitor.

Harry sobered. "Actually, Heather says she hopes this trip will help give Daisy a little polish that's badly needed. She's counting on you to be an example."

"I?" Delicate pink again swept to her brow.

"I cannot imagine a finer example of all that's admirable in a young woman than you, Miss Daphne."

Theodore Radcliffe's mouth closed so quickly it seemed impossible he had given the high compliment.

Harry and Alice exchanged glances, then she said, "I believe you were going to tell us of Daisy's latest escapade, dear."

Daphne breathed a sigh of relief. Tactful Mother, to step in and turn a rapidly worsening situation around.

"Oh, yes. Well, it seems my only niece couldn't constrain herself when our invitation arrived. She climbed into a fir tree, all but ruined a dress with pitch, rode a branch down like a horse when it broke off with her, and generally disgraced herself."

A sparkle of fun lit the guest's face. "She sounds like a very interesting person."

"Oh, she's that, all right. Just wait until you meet her."

Why should Father's words cast a pall over her own anticipation of Daisy's coming? Daphne couldn't explain the sudden touch of dread that darkened the bright room for a moment. All during the evening while Mother plied bright knitting needles in a soft, rosy mass of wool and Father read the paper, the blue-clad girl had to make an effort to talk with Theodore.

"Are you troubled about your cousin's coming?" he asked under cover of a stirring rendition by Beethoven.

"Oh, no. I love her. I've never had a friend who took her place and Daisy writes that all these years it's been the same with her. It's just that. . . ," she hesitated. She couldn't proclaim the truth that had hit her when Theodore showed interest! "No one can explain what she's like. You'll have to meet her, as Father said." Yet some of the glow surrounding the visit had dimmed and when he'd gone and the family devotions ended, Daphne slowly walked up the stairs to her own room. For the first time she felt glad Mother insisted Daisy be given the adjoining room, instead of sharing her daughter's.

"They may stay several weeks," she'd pointed out. "We have the space now that you're the only child left at home. You'll be more comfortable so."

"Father," Daphne prayed after she slipped into a cool nightdress and opened her window wide to the still-warm air. "I don't think I'm envious. I never felt jealous of Daisy before. Is it—Theodore?" She heard the quiver in her voice but struggled on. "I want him to like her, truly, Lord. Is it hateful to hope he doesn't like her better than he does me?" She stayed awake for a long time, facing her heart and conscience. Just before she fell asleep she whispered, "If it by Thy will, Lord, I don't want him to like anyone better than me." The night wind softly swayed the sheer curtains and cooled her face, and she slept.

Sometime in the night she awakened. Great white stars peered down on the silent world. Had a sound aroused her? Daphne lay perfectly still but nothing seemed to be out of the ordinary except her new awareness of young womanhood and how dear Theodore Radcliffe had grown. Her pulse quickened. She relived that moment when she'd seen a flicker in his eyes, more positive now that it had been real. A smile curved her lips. How outrageous of Father to treat their guest as one of the family. Yet if what she hoped came true, one day Theodore might be just that.

The curtains fluttered until they looked like wraiths dancing in the air currents. Memories from years gone by rippled with them.

*Someday we will live on a ranch and marry cowboys.* Daisy's secret dream, shared with no one on earth but Daphne. *Someday we'll ride horses up mountains and across sagebrush plains and into green valleys with rushing streams.*

Daphne could almost hear her cousin's voice, sketching a future they would share, one in which they'd never be separated again. She remembered how they'd clung to one another when she and her family left Washington; how Daisy's skinny arms clutched and the way she bent close and whispered in her ear, "Don't forget. Promise?"

"I'll never forget. Ever." Childish vows, yet not taken lightly. Even all these years later, uneasiness crept over Daphne and touched her with butterfly wings of doubt.

"I haven't forgotten, but I've outgrown those dreams," she softly told the listening night. "Daisy will have, too." Yet would she? What if her beloved cousin still planned to one day make her dreams come true—and counted on Daphne to help her?

The restless girl never really slept for the remainder of the night. Time after time she drowsed, dreamed of Daisy's reproachful face and her accusation, "You broke faith with me and I trusted you." She awakened to laugh and reassure herself then dreamed variations of the same thing again until Mother's call released her from spectres that fled before the rising sun.

After the morning meal while Alice and her daughter

planned happy times for their visitors, Daphne found her attention wandering. Out of a clear sky and apropos of nothing she asked, "Mother, do you think Theodore l-likes me?"

Alice gave no sign that she heard the breathlessness in the question. A sweet smile and candid blue eyes lit her face. "My darling, I believe he likes you much more than he can admit, even to himself." A reminiscent look further softened her expression. "I also believe it will take something unseen to give him the courage to speak. Do you want him to?"

"Very much." Daphne buried her face in her hands. "I keep seeing him with me as you are with Father—together, living and loving and being blessed with children."

"He's a fine man. I respect him more because he will never want anything from life more than loving you and serving God. He reminds me of Harry, in some ways."

"Really?" Daphne's eyes rounded in surprise. "Why, they're complete opposites. Father's so—so—and Theodore's so—"

Alice's laugh sounded like a chime of silvery bells and her daughter couldn't help joining in. "Yes, they are. But each is a man a woman can trust with her life and happiness."

"I feel this way, too. Mother, is that why you could leave your family and go with the Mercer expedition, all those thousands of miles away?"

"Yes, and I never regretted it. I hope and pray you and Theodore will always be close and since he's interested in the business, it may come to pass. If not, we'll know God's plan for each of our lives is best." She brushed a crystal drop from one eye and resumed her usual briskness. "Now, let's get back to our planning."

"I can hardly wait to see Daisy. It doesn't sound as if she's changed much." A little voice deep in her heart cried, *Oh, but I hope she's changed some. I don't want to ever live on a ranch and marry a cowboy. I want to stay right her in Kansas City and be Mrs. Theodore Radcliffe.* She hastily averted her face to keep her mother's keen eyes from noticing the bright red she felt climb into her hot cheeks and dutifully went about helping the servants who made her home so comfortable and lovely. If a little fear stayed with her no one knew but God.

&.

Brushed and waiting, Heather and Daisy felt the clanging wheels that had carried them so far across such a wide, changing country slow and at last stop. Panic seized the courageous Westerner who had faced danger and conquered all the adverse aspects of her Washington home. A glimpse from the window at crowds of people waiting for passengers to alight further disturbed her. She gripped her mother's gloved hand. "Good thing Father had us get these suits, isn't it?" Once started, she couldn't stop chattering. "I don't see anyone dressed nicer, although some of the ladies' gowns are different, and—"

"Do be still, Daisy." Heather squeezed her hand and smiled. "We'll be off in a minute and everything will be fine."

"You always understand, don't you?"

"I try. Oh, there's Harry!" She waved. "He didn't see me. Come on. We're here." She grasped her reticule with her free hand and motioned for Daisy to do the same, then stood and stepped into the aisle.

For one quivering moment her daughter cravenly wished herself back in the fir tree. She'd risk her father's anger all over, if necessary; it couldn't be worse than following Ma-Mother to meet relatives who loomed more frightening than a bear with cubs. Somehow, she managed to stumble after Heather and step down from the train, assisted by the porter.

"There they are!" An unmistakable treble voice, clear and with a hint of laughter, rang out. The next thing Daisy knew, soft arms encircled her. Delicate perfume assailed her nostrils and Daphne held her off to look at her. "You can't know how I've waited for this."

The visitor looked into the frank blue eyes and found her playmate. Stylish she might be, grownup and pretty, the child Daphne peeked out from between curling lashes above rosy cheeks. Daisy felt she had suddenly come home.

An older edition flew from Heather's arms and seized the bewildered guest. "You must stay all summer, if you can," she hospitably invited. "We have so many things planned. Your cousins all want to entertain you and of course, there's the church social and the box dinner and—"

A hazel-eyed man stepped forward, one arm around his twin. "There, Alice, let's get them home before we start the round you've laid out. Goodness, Daisy, you're even prettier than when I came to Washington."

She warmed to his approval and resemblance to his twin. "Thank you." But she instinctively turned back to Daphne as the daisies in the meadow at home turned toward the sun. "I'm so glad we came." Her spontaneous reply swept away any lingering feeling of strangeness. Even their arrival at the Templeton home with its splendor far beyond anything she'd seen couldn't faze her. As long as Daphne hadn't changed except on the outside, she need not fear. Caught up in the promised shopping spree that netted her more lovely gowns than Daisy felt she could ever use, along with shoes, undergarments, and hats, a side she hadn't known she possessed blossomed. A dozen times she prayed the sin of vanity wouldn't overtake her, then promptly forgot false pride and simply enjoyed wearing the new clothing.

Dinners, parties, and church followed, each offering insight into Kansas City life. Daisy wisely followed her more experienced cousin's lead in polite society with only a few mishaps, such as being too forthright with a smitten young man and stating she once had a pet dog that followed her around everywhere she went just the way he did. When Daphne heard of the incident she gently pointed out it had hurt the suitor's feelings, but she couldn't help giggling when her cousin demanded, "Why? It's true."

A week passed. Another. Daisy burned to talk about their longheld dreams but the flurry of activities left little time for girlish confidences. Intrigued as she was, sometimes Daisy longed for mountain and stream forest and valley. How could anyone ever be happy to live in Kansas City, interesting as it was? The social scene also disturbed her. Unused to late nights, afternoon teas, and the like, her soul felt shriveled and shrunken. Walking in the garden offered as much activity as many of the crowd that swarmed to the Templetons apparently desired. Daisy longed to run and climb and fill her lungs with clean, fresh air.

A cancelled engagement when rain spoiled plans for an outing finally opened the way to a good long talk. Fortified with plates of cookies, apples, and cheese, the girls parked on Daphne's bed and prepared to make up for all the time they'd missed.

Daisy bent a stern gaze on her cousin, soft and dainty in a simple white muslin afternoon dress. Her own pale yellow dimity skirts spread around her. "'Fess up," she ordered in her old imperative way. "That Radcliffe man's in love with you, isn't he?"

"His name's Theodore," Daphne mildly answered but her cousin noticed how her eyes shone.

"Why don't people call him Ted or Teddy?"

"He isn't at all a Ted or Teddy," Daphne defended and sat up straight. "His name means `gift of God'. Isn't that beautiful?" She sank back against a feather pillow.

"Y-es. So Long as he isn't a gift of God to you. We have other plans," she reminded. Face glowing, Daisy told how she'd seen the cowboy silhouetted against the early sunset atop the hill; he'd strengthened her belief that one day she would live on a ranch and marry a rider.

"Oh, Daisy, you still have that dream?"

The dismay in the question jolted the dreamer back to reality. She jerked erect and stared at Daphne's troubled face. "Of course! Didn't we always plan to—"

"We were only children," Daphne protested. Her face twisted.

Daisy felt she'd been hit with a falling tree. "You mean—but you promised. You said you wouldn't forget. Ever."

"I haven't forgotten. I just don't want that life now." A fresh set of tears drenched the blue eyes and pain crept into them. "I've hoped and prayed you had changed."

"While I hoped and prayed you hadn't." It sounded dull, even to her own ears. "It's Theodore, isn't it?"

"Yes." Daphne bowed her head. "I can't go away and leave him. He's the dearest person on earth."

Daisy's soft heart put aside bitter disappointment. She said huskily, "Then you mustn't feel bad about-about us. Mama says it's right for a woman to love her husband best."

"I'm so sorry," Daphne cried.

"Here, you're getting all red and splotchy." Daisy produced a clean handkerchief and handed it over. "Blow your nose and don't worry. Things will be all right." Yet she wondered how they could be. All these years, knowing Daphne shared her dream. It would take a long time to forget them.

*No!* Her inner self protested. "It may still be right for me, even if it isn't for you," she slowly said.

"How?" Daphne put aside her sodden handkerchief. Doubt widened her eyes but a little gleam also sparked there.

"I don't know." Daisy flung herself back on her pillow, hands clasped behind her head. She sighed. "I guess if it's what I should do, something will happen to make me know."

Yet days dragged by and nothing unusual occurred. No voices or miraculous offers of positions came to confirm the belief her dream would come true. One day she told God maybe she'd been wrong all through the years. Soon Daddy planned to come take them home. "It will mean the end of everything," she solemnly prayed. "Is that what You want?"

The very next afternoon Daphne bounced in looking mysterious. She put her finger over her lips for silence and beckoned Daisy to follow upstairs to her room. Inside, with the heavy door closed, she pulled a piece of paper from her dress pocket. "Just you wait until you see what I have," she gloated.

"A torn piece of paper, probably from a newspaper." Why should her cousin's behavior send thrills through the guest?

"Have you ever heard of Fred Harvey?"

Daisy tried to concentrate. "No-yes-oh, wasn't he that man who built the restaurants by the railroad?"

"Yes, and he used young women between eighteen and thirty as waitresses along the Atchison, Topeka & Sante Fe rail line."*

"Who cares?" Daisy shrugged her shoulders and patted a yawn.

"You, for one, should. You want to see ranches and cowboys and horses and cattle, don't you?" Daphne's eyes glittered.

"You know that I do, but I can't see—"

Her tormentor didn't let her finish. "And more than

---

*Fred Harvey died in 1901 but his program continued.

any other place, you want to see Arizona Territory, don't you?"

Daisy's spine straightened and she nodded.

"Then here's your chance if your parents will allow it. There's such a great shortage of women in Arizona, Harvey's is accepting Kansas girls and women to work in the establishments.

"They're in Kingman and Williams, Winslow and Ash Fork and Seligman. Daisy." Her teeth chattered with excitement. "There's a brand new four-story, log and rock building called El Tovar just back from the south rim of the Grand Canyon!"

# five

Daisy's mouth fell open in amazement. Could gentle Daphne, law-abiding except when led astray, actually be suggesting that—

"You'll make a perfect Harvey Girl, you know." Laughter twinkled in her blue eyes. "They have to be— and I quote—'of good moral character, attractive, intelligent and between eighteen and thirty.'"

"I've never waited table in my life," Daisy expostulated even while the familiar excitement that preceded a new caper licked through her veins.

"'No experience necessary,'" Daphne quoted triumphantly.

"What are you trying to do? Get rid of me?"

"You know better than that." Her cousin frowned. "I'm simply trying to think of a *respectable* way to help make your dreams come true now that I—well—"

"Now that Theodore has come into your life."

"Yes." She'd never looked prettier than with the wild rose color dancing in her cheeks.

Daisy curiously changed the subject. "What's it like, being in love?"

Knowledge far beyond her years crept into Daphne's eyes but she said promptly, "Wanting to be with him all the time, missing him when we aren't together, feeling thankful God allowed me to meet him." She hesitated and faltered. "He-he hasn't spoken. What if he doesn't care?"

"Then he is demented." Daisy hugged her. "Any man who doesn't fall in love with you is mad."

"Someday you'll meet the right one and when you do, you'll find happiness you haven't dreamed existed." Daphne straightened her shoulders. "Now about the Harvey Eating Houses."

"I'm not sure I care to tackle anything this stupendous," she admitted.

"What? The girl who kidnapped a papoose, eavesdroped from a fir—"

"Please. Those things happened when I was a mere child." She haughtily tilted her chin. "It *would* be a way to see the West, especially Arizona." Her hazel eyes glistened. "Who was this Fred Harvey, anyway? He must have had high standards or he wouldn't have required his waitresses to be of good character."

"He was beyond reproach. It's said 'Fred's Girls' are doing as much to settle the West by bringing culture as the pioneers who are settling it. If it weren't for Theodore, I'd be tempted to go with you." She sounded a bit wistful.

"Would you?" Daisy all but pounced on her. "What fun we'd have and Daddy and Ma-Mother would be much more inclined to let me go." A warning bell sounded in her brain. "Don't say a word about this until we find out more, will you?"

"Of course not. You'll need all the ammunition you can get before telling Uncle Brian and Aunt Heather what you want to do." She shook her head. "I'm sorry, but I

just can't go away for so long. Harvey Girls sign con-
tacts for a whole year." She sighed and Daisy had a
feeling Daphne put childhood things behind her and became a woman at that exact moment.

"If a person did want to be a Harvey Girl, what would
she do?"

Daphne rattled the torn newspaper piece. "It says to
write to "Harvey," in care of the Kansas City, Missouri
Union Depot."

"Why, that's just across the river!" Daisy's heart
bounced like a buckboard on a skid road. "What else
does it say?" Her fingers itched to snatch the page and
read for herself. Instead, she must wait for Daphne's
maddening perusal of the information before she passed
it on.

"You have to furnish a signed statement that you won't
get married for a year." She giggled. "The way I hear
it, there are so few nice women out West, Harvey's know
they had best tie up the girls. It has a right to, though.
Remuneration is $25.00 or more a month and when you
add in tips, room, board and travel it's good wages."
She fixed a stern gaze on her cousin. "Dear girl, if you
should decide to marry before the year's up, remember
this: Harvey's holds back half your first year's salary if
you do."

"Marry? I? When there is so much to see and do?
Don't be a goose," Daisy declared.

"So you are interested, after all," Daphne twitted.

"If I can't go, I think I'll die." The guest clasped hands
to her bosom and pretended to swoon.

"I wouldn't tell your parents that. It's going to take

all the skill you have at wheedling to get their blessing," Daphne wisely reminded.

"Then I won't tell them—I mean, until I'm accepted." The idea grew like Mr. Phinney's famous turnip.

*"What?"*

"What sense does it make to get people het up unless I'm sure I will be chosen?" Daisy demanded, hands on hips and arms akimbo. "I'd be humiliated if I talked Daddy and Mama into this and then a letter come and said, 'My dear Miss O'Rourke, we want Kansas maidens, not backwoods young women from Washington State.' Oh dear," she wailed, sounding more like nine than nineteen. "I'm not cultured and polished. They'll never take me in a hundred, thousand, million years!"

"Now who's being a goose?" Daphne's soft white hand stroked the tumbled red curls. "Besides, you're smart enough to learn, aren't you?"

"You think I could?" Unworthiness forgotten, Daisy's face opened like a flower to the sun.

"Why not? I don't see you have that much to learn and what you do, I can teach you. Really, Daisy, once you control your impulsive jumping in before you find out how deep things are, you'll be fine."

"I think so, too, if I'm just given the chance." A brooding look shadowed her expressive face. "Daphne, how would you like to have a visitor for a longer time? Do you think Aunt Alice and Uncle Harry will let me stay after Daddy comes and takes Mama home?" Intent on her new brainstorm, she forgot to say *Mother,* which she personally considered more elegant.

"I'd love to have you stay as long as you can," cried

her co-conspirator. "How are you going to get permission?"

Daisy's fertile mind already held ideas that sprang to life. "I'll tell them the truth. Since I came here and saw how ladylike you are, I've decided I should be more like you. It's true. I just won't say why." The plan unrolled like General Sherman's battle strategy. "My deportment will improve until they'll see what a good thing a few more weeks can be." She leaped up, executed a wide dance guaranteed to turn Indian war dancers forest-green with envy, and collapsed on Daphne's bed.

"Were you speaking of deportment, Miss O'Rourke?" Daphne reminded ominously.

"My stars, I'll have to let off steam when we're alone or I'll explode like a teakettle with a plugged spout, won't I?"

A week later Brian arrived in Kansas City, expecting to be met by a whirlwind. He looked amused when a proper young lady minced toward him, smiled, and said, "It is good to see you, Father."

Daisy immediately backslid enough to give him a hug but her grueling self-improvement campaign had already begun to show results. She kept her voice well modulated instead of allowing it to rise when she grew excited. She showed extra consideration of her mother until Heather frankly confessed she felt smothered and sent her hovering daughter away to find Daphne. Yet a day or two before time for them to depart, the hoyden-turned-lady approached her parents and said simply,

"May I stay longer? The Templetons are willing and I feel I could benefit greatly from the advantages of

learning about places other than Arizona." She saw the
dismayed look the two she loved best in the world exchanged and pressed the point. "Daphne is so wonderful about helping me improve. Wouldn't you like for me
to come home a better and more learned person?"

"We'll discuss it," was the only answer she received
but a certain little smile on her father's merry lips hinted
at possible good news and she unobtrusively crossed her
fingers behind her back, rejecting the idea of wheedling.
Not this time when she stood at a crossroads. She'd
prayed about it—a lot. If her growing desire and excitement meant God approved, her way lay clear. A few
times she considered the fact it would be extremely dif-
ficult to differentiate between God's will and her own
"I-hope-God-will" feelings but quickly put the thoughts
away. Even proper Daphne had admitted how a Christian young woman serving as a Harvey Girl might be
given opportunities to witness to those she met.

The following morning brought blazing sun and ec-
stasy. Brian soberly told his only daughter that after much
consideration, he and Heather had decided to grant her
request. "Not that we ever want to lose the Washington
State Daisy," he said. "We do, however, admire some
of the new traits and the obvious restraint you are at-
tempting to use in curbing impulses."

Guilt smote her even while a little voice inside ar-
gued, *Being a Harvey Girl isn't an impulse. Haven't I
read and studied and prayed about it ever since I heard
about them?* Still, her lips trembled at the railway station when she bid her parents good-bye. If things went
as she planned, she would also be taking a train in a few

weeks—but not to Seattle—and more than a year would pass before she saw her parents' dear faces again. The thought came closer to breaking her determination than anything else so far. She opened her mouth to cry out for the train, already starting to chug its way along the tracks, to stop so she could board. The words stilled when Brian called, "Goodbye, mavourneen. We're proud of you."

Throat clogged with tears and shame, she could only wave and cling to Daphne until the train *clickety-clacked* out of sight. They stood until the engine and cars became only a memory, then red-eyed and weeping, Daisy muttered, "I will make them proud of me" and marched to the waiting carriage for their ride back to the Templetons, which had become her second home.

Once inside the massive doors, gloom fled. She had chosen, now she'd look ahead, not back. Daisy threw herself into learning to be a lady with all the ardor of youth and her strong-willed heritage. "It isn't that different from what Mother did," she earnestly tried to convince Daphne, who had swung from enthusiasm to a dubious, more realistic view of the enterprise. "She ran away from her father and step-mother."

Flaxen curls shook in violent disagreement. "Be honest with yourself. The situations are nothing alike. Your grandfather threatened to put Aunt Heather in an institution. You just long for adventure." Her mood lightened. "Not that I blame you. If Theodore doesn't hurry up and declare himself or ask Father for my hand, I might just—no, I won't." She looked sheepish and Daisy laughed, a clear brook-like trill.

One day her mentor declared, "You're as ready as you need to be. It's time for you to write your letter of application."

"Mercy, what will I say?" Daisy turned pale at the prospect.

"Read the qualifications again and answer accordingly," Daphne advised.

A flurry of ink-stained pages fell to the carpet like giant snowflakes before Daisy submitted her letter for approval.

Daphne read it out loud. "You catch errors or awkward places better that way," she commented.

"Dear sirs: I wish to be considered for a position in one of your Arizona Harvey Houses. I am nineteen-years-old, in excellent health and am willing to work hard. I come from a strong, Christian family and have never been questioned as to my character. I am certainly not beautiful, but I am pleasant looking, 5'6" and about 120 lbs and strong enough to serve the hours necessary to do the job. I hope you do not consider me impertinent, but if you have an opening at the Grand Canyon in Williams this would be my first choice. However, I will go where most needed. Thank you for your response.

"I'm not sure about asking for specific places," Daphne told her. "I guess it won't hurt, especially since you added that about not being impertinent and being willing to go where he needs you."

"I thought I might as well ask. Oh, Daphne, it will be almost like heaven if I'm accepted." Daisy wiped a film of perspiration from her forehead, warmed by both the hot day and the exertion of saying just the right thing in her letter.

"How long do you think it will take to get a reply? Will they call me in for an interview?"

"I don't think so. I think they just select from the applications. Now all we have to do is wait." She grinned. "I'm good at that. I've given Theodore Radcliffe ever so many opportunities to speak and he hasn't."

Daisy, usually sympathetic, remained caught up in her own schemes and merely nodded.

"Don't forget to add *very truly yours* before you sign it," Daphne called after her when she took the letter and started back to her own room to address an envelope.

"I won't." Yet minutes after she sat down in a comfortable chair in a room grown familiar and dear, the applicant sat and stared at her letter. It wasn't too late to turn back. All she had to do was tear up the letter and swear Daphne to ever-lasting secrecy.

"Never!" She bounded to her feet at the preposterous idea. Give up her dreams, now that she had come so close? Why, just the idea of wasting all those hours of learning to overcome her natural bent for mischief appalled her. Stored memories gleaned from rare photographs and magazine pictures tantalized and tempted: red rock canyons and pinnacles; green valley floors dotted with rusty-red and white cattle; horses; a long, low ranch house; a dusty cowboy with a white-toothed wide grin and love in his eyes riding in at the end of day.

She contrasted the scenes with home scenes and they failed by comparison. Surely there would be evergreen trees in northern Arizona, brooks, and slopes to climb, wildflowers. Best of all, she'd experience adventures beyond what Washington, dear as it was, offered.

Daisy sat down again and picked up her pen. She obediently wrote the *very truly yours* and admired how business-like it looked at the end of her clear writing. Nothing fancy in the way she made the letters but plenty of character in their firm strokes. Did Harvey's judge by the handwriting? If so, she had no problem.

Another reading of the letter disclosed an alarming fact. She hadn't said one word about not being from Kansas. *Don't,* a sneaky voice advised her brain. *Isn't that why you spent all those hours learning to be a second Daphne Templeton, so you could erase any sign of uncivilized behavior that might disqualify you?*

"It's Daphne who should be applying," Daisy soberly told herself. "She's the real lady. I'm just make-believe." Doubts assailed her. At first she laughed them off but they persisted, licking away at her newly won self-confidence like deer at a salt lick. "I know I can do it if they will just take me," she whispered in the stillness of the drowsy, late afternoon heat. She raised her pen again, touched it to the page, formed a capital *D* then glared at it. She could just imagine a supercilious Harvey's clerk opening her letter, looking down his long nose, and reading the name *Daisy O'Rourke.* Why, he'd probably throw the application in the trash without ever reading that its owner possessed all the qualities desirable for a Harvey Girl, many of them hard won.

Her thoughts whirled on until Daphne stuck her head in the doorway and reminded, "If we're to get your letter posted, you'd best hurry."

"All right." Daisy turned the corner of her lips down, resisted the temptation to discard her letter, and once more took up the pen. Heart pounding, she rapidly added the necessary signature, blotted it, and slid it into an envelope. A few more strokes and she finished. "For better or for worse," she muttered. Catching up a parasol to shade her from the sun, she slipped her letter into a pocket of the light green summer gown that just skimmed the top of her dainty white slippers and ran humming down the stairs to meet her cousin and speed the epistle on its way.

The days of waiting felt endless. Every time the girls left the house they came back anxious to see if Daisy had received a response. She alternated between the highest hopes and darkest despair. A dozen times she sadly said, "They won't take me." On every such occasion her partner in the situation loyally told her Harvey's wouldn't dare turn down such a fine candidate. Daphne also planned a round of social activities, visits to museums and shops and kept her distracted guest as busy as possible.

They came in laughing one late afternoon to meet a curious Alice and bewildered Harry. Daisy's heart leaped to her throat and her mouth went dry when he held up a letter.

"Daphne, why would you be receiving correspondence from Harvey's? I know they're recruiting waitresses, but where did they get your name?"

"I don't know," she truthfully answered. "It probably isn't important." She carelessly took the envelope and stuffed it in the reticule she carried while shopping. "We'd

best wash up, Daisy. It must be almost time for dinner."
Laughing and chatting she led the way upstairs, with her
cousin following, and took out the letter.

"Isn't it funny?" she asked when they reached Daisy's
bedroom "You apply for a position and I get recruited.
Dear me, how did they ever—and look, isn't it odd? The
envelope is addressed to Miss D. Templeton." She
started to slit it with her fingernail but Daisy's faint
voice stopped her.

"It-it's mine."

"Yours?" Daphne looked thunderstruck. "How can it
be?"

Daisy hadn't felt so small for years. "Daphne, I-I
thought they'd think Daisy O'Rourke sounded like a stage
girl." She bit her lips and felt the blood drain from her
face. "When I sent the application, I signed it *D.
Templeton.*"

The unopened letter fell to the floor between them.
Daphne turned ghastly. "You didn't. You couldn't have.
Daisy. . ." She couldn't go on.

"It's not a lie," the culprit said meekly. "I *am* D.
Templeton. I just left off the O'Rourke." For a moment
Daphne's frozen stance frightened her. What had she
done? She glanced down, unable to meet the accusing
gaze. Hope fluttered its wings. She snatched the letter
from the carpet and ripped it open. "Maybe things aren't
so bad. Perhaps the application's rejected."

"What does it say?" Daphne regained the power of
speech and color returned to her face.

Daisy laughed, a croaking, mirthless sound. Her face
reddened and a little sob followed.

*"Well?"*

"I-we-you're accepted. My-our-your railway pass to Williams, Arizona is enclosed." She hated herself for the joy that burst inside her when Daphne looked so stricken. "I'm sorry," she managed to choke out. "I just wanted it so much. Daphne, please, don't look at me like that." She held out pleading arms, begging for the understanding she always received from the faithful one who never let her down. The chill of shock withstood her belated repentance, if singing in Daisy's heart mixed with fright at what she'd done could be called such.

Daphne stepped back and held out both hands to ward off weakening. "This time you've gone too far. Don't you know I'll be the laughing-stock of Kansas City?" she furiously demanded. "Daisy Templeton O'Rourke, you got me into this mess and this time you're going to get me out of it. What do you think Father and Mother will say?" Tears of anger sprang to her blue eyes like thunder clouds leaped into blue Puget Sound Skies. She pressed a shaking hand to her mouth and added, "I can never face Theodore again as long as I live!" She whipped around and ran out, leaving Daisy mute and without excuse.

# six

Daphne sat through dinner, silent and making no pretense to eat. Daisy did little better. When Harry raised his eyebrows at the unusual silence, Alice shook her head at him but following dessert, left untouched by the girls, she suggested, "Perhaps we should go into the parlor and discuss what's evidently bothering you two."

Her daughter answered in a tone cold enough to freeze a polar bear, "Perhaps we should." The look she gave Daisy boded no good and with a determination she hadn't known she possessed, she refused to offer even one comforting glance. The thought of what Theodore Radcliffe would think further strengthened her. This was no childish prank with guilt to be equally born. Daisy had to learn someday she couldn't rush headlong into trouble, be sorry, and gain instant forgiveness. Every time Daphne looked at her bosom companion's misery, she felt fiercely glad. Let her suffer the way her innocent victim was bound to do, once word got out about the name change, as it surely would. *Be sure your sin will find you out,* * rang in her weary brain. A dozen, nay, a hundred times Mother and Aunt Heather had quoted the scripture to their wayward offspring. Daphne tossed her blond head. This wasn't her sin, even if she would have to pay for it, she bitterly concluded.

---

*Numbers 32:23

76

"All right, girls, what seems to be the trouble?"

Daphne folder her arms and stared at her cousin, then dropped them and felt for the crackle of paper in the pocket of her gown. She had gone to Daisy's room and retrieved it after her cousin went down to dinner. "Ask her."

"I don't think we have to ask." Harry Templeton looked serious. "This has to do with the letter from Harvey's, doesn't it?"

"How did you know?" Daphne cried. Her anger increased.

He looked steadily at her, then turned an understanding but stern glance toward Daisy. "I've never known you to be together for long without getting into some kind of prank. We'd hoped now that you're grown up things might be different." The disappointment in his voice swept anger from his daughter's heart and she looked down to hide the tears she felt coming.

Daisy make a choked noise, clutched her hands into fists until the knuckles showed white, and squared her shoulders. "You mustn't blame Daphne." Her low voice still rang clear. "It's all my doing. She knew nothing of it. I mean, she knew I wanted to be a Harvey Girl and that I wrote a letter, but I signed *D. Templeton* because Daisy O'Rourke sounds like a stage name and I just had to get to see Arizona and it wasn't a lie, for my name really is D. Templeton if you leave off the O'Rourke—"

"That will do." Harry held up one hand to stop the torrent of words from his white-faced niece. Daphne saw his lips twitch and the relief in his hazel eyes. Strangely, it didn't make her feel much better.

"She-she's not all to blame," she faltered, knowing she must be fair. "She barely knew who Fred Harvey was and never heard of his chain of restaurants and lodging places until I brought home a clipping from the paper." She dug the toe of her slipper into the thick carpet and stared at it. "I-I encouraged her to apply and helped her be a lady and—" She clapped her hand to her mouth, but too late.

"Oh, you did, did you?" Mother's usual placid face set in the expression that warned of a coming storm. "May your Father and I be so bold as to ask why?"

Daphne felt crammed between walls slowly closing in on her. She couldn't very well explain she'd made the suggestion to compensate Daisy for going back on their childhood plans. That would involve explaining her feelings for Theodore. Neither could she betray her cousin's confidence. One look into the hazel eyes so like Father's showed anguish and a final plea for silence. To blurt out that Daisy had always wanted to live on a cattle ranch and marry a cowboy, preferably in Arizona, would be far more cruel punishment than she deserved.

She looked imploringly at Mother, whose round blue eyes slowly lost their glacial hue before she said, "We respect your loyalty to one another but we must get to the bottom of this."

Feeling like a criminal, Daphne stubbornly set her lips, wondering where her rage had flown. She saw defeat in Daisy's expression and the awareness of one another they'd always shared whispered a full confession hung ready to be uttered. Once the words were spoken, they would brand their speaker as a willful child, in spite of her nineteen years, and shatter any chance of her dream coming true.

"We decided there was no reason to say anything to Uncle Brian and Aunt Heather," Daphne hurriedly began. "What if Daisy didn't get accepted? Everyone would get upset over nothing. About her using my name—she didn't lie. She just didn't tell all the truth."

"I presume you did plan to tell your parents before you actually left Kansas City?" Alice asked Daisy.

Horrified color swept into her face. "Of course. Please believe me, Aunt Alice." She clasped her hands loosely in front of her chest. "I know I'm heedless and shouldn't have applied without telling Mama and Daddy, but, I *have* to see more than Washington!" Her eyes glittered. "There's a whole world and I'm getting older all the time. This seemed the only way. The Harvey Girls are respected everywhere they serve. They're chaperoned and watched over as carefully as you watch over Daphne. Don't you see? This is my only chance to get away!" Her impassioned words stayed in the air.

Alice and Harry looked into each other's faces. Daphne had the feeling they were remembering back over the years to other girls, one younger than Daisy, who refused to fit into the pattern laid out before them. Of a young man who left home at an even earlier age. She tensed, wondering if the memories would give them enough understanding to apply toward Daisy and be in sympathy with her.

Gradually, a twinkle began in her father's eyes and an answering spark appeared in Alice's. Harry turned to face his niece, still standing before him waiting the judgement. "I don't know what your parents will say to all this, but if you feel it will help, I'll put a word in for you."

"So will I." Alice looked stern. "We don't approve of the way you've chosen to get what you want, but you're a young woman, not a child. If a taste of the frontier is what it takes for you to be happy, then perhaps you should have it."

For a single moment Daisy remained where she was. Then a white flame swept into her face. In a tornado rush, she ran and embraced first Harry, then Alice. She paused before Daphne. "Can you ever forgive me?"

The radiance in her face went straight to Daphne's tender heart. "I already have," she softly replied and opened her arms.

To all appearances, an hour later the Templeton household had settled back into its normal routine, except for a subdued Daisy who wouldn't know her fate until an answer came to the telegram Uncle Harry sent off immediately. She had no way of knowing just what he said but could certainly imagine the consternation its arrival in Washington would bring.

Daphne excused herself and slipped down to the library for a book. She would read herself to sleep and perhaps forget the heaviness that still lay on her heart. Things might work out for Daisy, but what about her? An unusual rebellion arose. If Theodore let a paltry thing like a girlish trick lower his esteem for her—providing he had any—who cared?

"I do," she told the musty volumes. "If I had the courage I'd do something drastic. Didn't Mother say it would

take an unexpected happening to make him speak? If
only I knew what." She paced the carpeted floor, her
soft slippers making no sound and her skirts but a slight
swishing noise. Why couldn't she think of a scheme? "I
could ask Daisy for help but mercy! We'd be in a worse
pickle than we are now." A faint crackle reminded her
the new Harvey Girl's acceptance still lay in her pocket.
Her fingers absently drew it out. In the dim light stream-
ing from the open door to the parlor, she traced the address with a shapely, white finger. *Miss D. Templeton.*
How official it sounded.

The kernel of an idea dropped into her searching brain.
Did she dare? Could she get away with it? Perspiration
sprang to her forehead along with a plan so nefarious as
to put all Daisy's plots to shame. She rejected it. Temptation came back and brought its seven brothers. An
impish grin formed on her sweet lips; she laughed. What
had Daisy said? "It wasn't a lie. . .my name really is D.
Templeton."

"Daddy and Mama always taught me good could come
out of everything, Lord," she whispered. "Would it be a
sin if I helped it along—just a little?"

For three days she considered, keeping her own counsel. A dozen times she longed to ask Daisy's advice but
refrained. Even if she were willing to outline her plan,
the silence between Kansas City and Seattle prevented
it. The strain of waiting for a reply to the telegram showed
in a pair of hazel eyes that often held a faraway look
mingled with despair.

Theodore Radcliffe called one evening, bringing a
paper Harry had inadvertently left at the office, one he

needed in order to complete some work at home. Alice had gone out to a church committee meeting. Daisy lay on her bed upstairs, simply waiting and enduring.

"Daphne, take Theodore into the parlor, maybe have some music. I have to complete this task." Harry rumpled his hair and headed for the library.

Her time had come, one of the few occasions on which she could be alone with the man she loved. "Would you excuse me just for a moment?" she told her guest.

"Of course." He looked surprised but his nice blue eyes couldn't hide delight at the prospect of an exclusive visit with her. It gave Daphne courage for what lay ahead.

Hope fixed wings to her feet and she sped upstairs, took the letter from Harvey's she kept buried among her laces and collars, and put it into her pocket. It gave off a comforting crackle that sent red flags flying in her pretty face. Her heart marched in time with the feet that barely touched the stair treads on the way down.

Theodore had remained standing in the pleasant parlor with its furniture fresh and sparkling in summer covers and the scent of roses delicately perfuming the air. From the open windows rose the sleepy songs of birds suddenly aware they were up past their bedtime.

"Miss Daphne, you're looking well. As if something particularly nice has happened to you." Theodore's shy smile and compliment once he'd seated her and taken a chair across from her turned the young woman's face the color of the brightest red roses. It also raised her ebbing determination to carry out her plan.

"Why, thank you." She slowly withdrew the letter from her pocket. "Something has happened." She couldn't bring herself to label it *nice*. "Would you like to read my letter?"

He looked a bit surprised but was too well-bred to exclaim. "If you wish me to read it." He took the envelope, smiled, and removed the page. The railway pass fell out first. Theodore glanced at it, then at her. "Why—"

"Please read the letter." Daphne thought she'd choke. For an instant she longed to snatch it back but already his bewildered blue gaze had turned to the letter. What had she done? Was this how Daisy always felt once her rocket went off, as if the stick had plunged down and into her heart?

She had little time for remorse. Letter, railway pass, and envelope flew in three directions. Theodore Radcliffe, galvanized into action by the plainly devastating news, bounded from his chair, crossed the space between them, and knelt at Daphne's feet. He took both her trembling hands in his. She hadn't known how strong they were until he pressed hers and burst out,

"You, a Harvey Girl? No! You can't leave Kansas City."

Even through pity for his paleness and distraught appearance, Daphne knew satisfaction. Her plan had worked beyond her wildest expectation. "Why, Theodore, what difference does it make to you who becomes a Harvey Girl?"

"The difference between happiness and continuing heartache," he flashed back. His eyes turned pure sapphire. "Daphne, I love you with all my heart. It's been all I could do to keep from telling you and I've had to remind myself your family is well-off while I'm just a clerk. I planned to wait until I received a promotion, but now, why, if you go away, life will be meaningless." In a fluid movement he stood, placed his hands on her shoulders and said, "Is it too much to hope that someday you might care for me?"

She looked into his eyes and saw herself reflected in their clear depths. "Someday? Theodore Radcliffe, I've cared ever so long and I—"

The touch of his lips effectively interrupted her.

A long and exquisite time later he released her enough to lead her to a low couch. One arm still around her, he murmured, "You won't go away, will you?"

It brought Daphne to her senses. "I never meant to."

"But the letter!" He looked at the scattered papers, then back at her.

"It's Daisy who is going, if her parents will agree. She applied as D. Templeton, which is her first initial and middle name."

"Then—Daphne, you deceived me?"

She hated the look of wounded pride that darkened his honest gaze. "I had to, Theodore. M-Mother said you needed something to encourage you to speak and I just couldn't wait any longer."

"You loved me that much?" He sounded incredulous.

"Y-yes. Can you ever forgive me" she quavered.

"You darling." He caught her close. She could feel his heart pound beneath her ear. "Thank God you had the courage to do what you've done." Daphne felt she'd completed a long, stormy voyage and sailed into a fair haven, a place of safety and joy. Let Daisy chase after her horses and cattle and cowboys, if that's what would make her happy. She wouldn't trade Theodore for all the lost gold mines in Arizona.

Daphne straightened, slid from her sweetheart's arms, and said, "Don't you want to talk with Father? Mother isn't here."

New manliness filled his quietly smiling face. "Yes. May I do it now?"

"Of course." Daphne called in her bell-like voice, "Father, Theodore and I have something to tell you." She squeezed his hand. "We'll do it together."

He placed a firm arm around her shoulders. "Just as we will be together until death do us part. God is so good."

Harry Templeton didn't act at all surprised at their news. His hazel eyes twinkled with mischief equal to Daisy's. "I figured someday you'd be part of the family, son. Welcome."

"I don't want any big wedding that takes months to plan," Daphne asserted. She smiled at her father from the security of her fiance's arms. "What I'd really like is a wedding before Daisy leaves so she can stand up with me." She laughed, a clear, ringing sound that spilled happiness into the room. "In a way, it's due to Daisy's gumption in going after what she wants. I wouldn't have had the daring or means without her." She raised her voice and called loudly enough for the sound to penetrate the upper hall and bedroom door. "Daisy, come down here at once and meet your new cousin-to-be!" She wanted to shout it from the church steeple until all of Kansas and Missouri knew. Theodore Radcliffe loved her and that made her the most blessed, joyous woman in the world. Now if only Daisy. . . She smiled at her desire for matchmaking.

Alice made no argument about a hasty wedding. Hadn't she traveled halfway around the world to reach Harry? Family and a few friends would nicely fill the parlor with the library doors thrown open for overflow. A morning wedding followed by a simple luncheon took care of the ceremony and reception. "Give us a few days to get gowns for you and Daisy," she told her ecstatic daughter. She bustled away to write the few necessary invitations, grieving that Heather and Brian wouldn't be there but practical in the extreme. By the time they could come, Daisy would be gone, for a long letter had arrived that brought both tears and delight.

"I can hardly believe it," Daisy had said through her dazed state. "Mama at first said absolutely not. Daddy paced the floor and said he'd not for being surprised at anything I did." Bright drops sparkled and fell. "The more they talked, the more they decided perhaps I needed to be away from them and you and on my own in order to grow up. They reminded me I am nineteen-years-old and should be woman enough to conduct myself in a way to make them proud. Uncle Harry." She turned gratefully to him. "They said all the endorsements you sent concerning the impeccable reputation of the entire Harvey House enterprises made a great impact on their decision. I really appreciate it."

"Just be the best waitress ever who served," he told her.

But even the pending trip took second place to Daphne's wedding. In her happiness, she was little help.

Now that Theodore had placed a small but perfect gold ring on her engagement finger, she walked around smiling into its tiny blue stone and chattering of domestic duties. The imposing Templeton home knew the whine of saws and clean, pounding strokes of nails as remodeling turned the entire west side into a cozy apartment with separate enclosed entrance. At first Theodore had acted doubtful, but when Harry and Alice frankly told him if he preferred, they would accept rent and apply it to the construction costs, he gave in. Perhaps he saw the desolate look in the Templetons' eyes at losing their last child and rattling around in the large home. In any event, Daphne walked through the days before her wedding in beauty and light.

Daisy watched her beloved cousin and benefited from the new maturity that came with the idea of being a wife. Never had Daphne been more beautiful or gentle, with her family and the servants, as well as Theodore. At times a little envy crept into Daisy's heart, although she thanked God for the happiness that flowed around her. Surely one day she would fully know the source of the look that sprang into Daphne's eyes when Theodore came or when she spoke of him.

"I never dreamed love would be like this," she said late one evening just before the wedding. She twisted her ring and perfect trust deepened the blue of her eyes. "Daisy, no matter what else you do in life, don't ever promise to marry a man unless you know with your whole heart he is the one God has sent into your life."

Daisy, like Mary in the Bible, tucked their conversation away and pondered it in her heart.

By a freak of chance, it turned out Daisy had to leave the same day Daphne became Mrs. Theodore Radcliffe. As soon as her maid of honor duties ended, she hastily folded her soft pale green gown into her overflowing trunk, donned the pretty dark blue traveling suit she'd worn to Kansas City, and hastened to the railway station. She insisted that none of the family accompany her. "This is Daphne's day and I will be perfectly all right," she said firmly, even when doubts crept up behind her. They attacked the minute the driver turned the corner and she could no longer see the Templeton home, which she'd learned to love. She comforted herself by opening her reticule and touching the railway pass and letter that had brought so much dismay and a declaration of love.

Daisy gasped. The letters danced in front of her eyes. In all the confusion of the engagement and wedding plans, not one of the family had remembered her papers were still as originally approved. Again, for better or for worse, of necessity Daisy O'Rourke would be known as D. Templeton.

## seven

In the time between Daphne's first mention of the Harvey
Girls and Daisy actually boarding the train for the long
tip south and west, she had reveled in the freedom waiting once she left Kansas City. A hundred times she had
visualized herself strolling down the aisle of the sway-
ing train, seating herself in the dining car and being completely on her own.

Alas and alack for such dreams. She discovered to
her dismay—and secret, unadmitted delight—at least an
even half-dozen other young women were on their way
to the Southwest, neophyte Harvey Girls no more experienced than she. Daisy quickly packed away her desire
for independence and joined wholeheartedly in the innocent fun. The girls gathered as much as possible and
once Kansas City lay behind, "Miss Templeton" confessed the D. stood for Daisy but said nothing of her
origins.

No one seemed to care. Kansas farm girls brushed
skirts with former seamstresses and those who frankly
stated they intended to find love and a husband in Arizona or New Mexico. "You'll have no trouble with
beaux except too many of them will be making calf eyes
at you," one merry companion warned.

"I supposed they'll ignore you," Daisy retorted to the
sparkling, diminutive brunette with black-pansy eyes.

She had been thrilled to learn Magnolia Symington would be one of the Williams Harvey Girls. Noley, as she called herself, retained most of the Southern accent she'd brought when her parents moved to Missouri years before but contradicted the stereotype of languid, Southern womanhood. Daisy suspected the tiny belle had been in much mischief during her life and she warmed to her new friend. No one could ever take Daphne's place but Mrs. Theodore Radcliffe had a new life and her cousin must move on to other friendships.

"I've heard all kinds of stories," Noley said, eyes flashing. "Why, did you know—if gossip is to be believed—the saloon women and dance hall girls hate the Harvey Girls. I heard that in many Western towns when the Harvey House is built, it takes business from the local establishments. Men come in to see the waitresses because they are ladylike. Anyway, the story says a dance hall queen decided to do something about it. She washed her face, put on decent clothing, and asked to see Fred Harvey, who at the time was in one of the Arizona Harvey Houses." She smiled, showing twin dimples and even white teeth. Her black eyes sparkled with fun. "She made up some story about a sad life and Mr. Harvey felt sorry for her, even though her application was irregular. He told her she could work for him; that he couldn't be even partly responsible for her having to take up the life of a fallen women like—and he gave *her name*." Her listeners gasped.

"What did she say?" Daisy demanded, feeling a little wicked at listening to such a risque story but eager to know the ending.

Noley raised a silky eyebrow. "According to what I heard, the phone applicant was supposed to have told him in no uncertain term, she was not fallen but had been pushed!" Laughter broke like a tree branch, spilling through the little band. "Can't you just imagine the proper Mr. Harvey's face when he realized to whom he was speaking? Oh, needless to say, she didn't get the job."

No group could get downhearted with Noley in its midst. Daisy felt herself expand and had to mentally remind Miss Templeton to watch what she said. A dozen times she nearly betrayed herself. Not through lack of manners. Daphne's teaching had been excellent and lasting. The finest array of silver and crystal couldn't faze her. As Kansas unrolled beneath the shining wheels and the group inevitable paired off in twos and threes, Daisy had time alone with Noley.

"Do you really plan to find a husband in Arizona?" she shyly asked her seatmate one hot afternoon when nothing but flat land and an occasional tumbleweed broke the monotony of the trip. Daisy found herself longing for trees and water, not distant blue pools the conductors told them were mirages.

"Oh, I do." Noley bounced on the seat and mysteriously lowered her voice. "The Missouri clodhoppeers are nice enough but not at all exciting."

"That's just the way I feel about the Washington loggers," Daisy blurted out. To her amazement Noley grinned and said,

"So that's why you talk differently." She cocked her shining dark head. "'Fess up. Are you ashamed of your state?"

"Of course not." Indignation raised Daisy's spirits that had plummeted to her toes when she realized how she'd given herself away. "I just didn't know if I could get the job as Daisy O'Rourke, and—"

Noley clapped her hands. "Daisy O'Rourke. It's perfect for you!" She leaned close. "I won't tell, even though I'm dying of curiosity. Why did you use the name Templeton? Who are your parents? Gracious, it took all my teasing to get Mama and Daddy to let me come. What were you doing in Kansas City, anyway?"

"You must promise not to give me away. I suppose they could say I signed the contract under false pretenses, except Templeton really is my name. My middle name and Mama's maiden name." She smiled. Since knowing Noley, the perfect lady, and hearing her say *Mama*, it now longer seemed important for Daisy to switch to the more formal *Mother*. "I hardly know where to start." She thought for a moment. "I suppose with a dream only one other person on earth knows." In descriptive phrases and growing passion she spread out her long-held desires to one day live on a cattle ranch and marry a cowboy.

Once Noley smiled and satisfaction filled her eager face. Daisy realized again how similar they were, in some ways even more than she and Daphne had been. Her cousin's dreams reflected her own when they were children, while the Southern girl's thoughts lived in a pioneering world of excitement even while her body stayed in Missouri.

The longer Daisy talked, the closer Noley bent until

their heads nearly touched, and when the story ended, the smaller girl echoed, "It's my story, too." Her white skin wore red streamers. "Daisy, I've felt so alone when no one could understand why I'd leave a perfectly good home and take up work they considered menial. I-I've actually prayed I'd find a friend who would realize this isn't just a whim."

"Are you a Christian, Noley?"

"Why, yes. Aren't you?" She looked astonished but at Daisy's quick nod, relaxed and said a strange thing. "If I didn't know God, do you think I'd have had the courage to stand against all my family and friends and go out to a place that may prove disappointing and not like my dreams at all?"

Two of the other Harvey Girls interrupted them before Daisy could reply, but she thought a lot about what Noley had said. Had she relied on God to see her through or simple chased off after a Western rainbow looking for an imaginary pot of gold? *I can't say I feel You are leading me, exactly,* she silently prayed. *I came on my own and because I felt I'd smother if I didn't break free. Please, in spite of my impetuousness, be with me.*

Flat land gave way to rolling hills with sagebrush and lazy tumbleweeds. Dust and heat prevailed but did little to dim the travelers' spirits. More Harvey Girls joined them in their trek West, climbing aboard with the same look of excited trepidation Daisy had felt in Kansas City. She, Noley, and the others did what they could to make the late additions to their merry company welcome. In New Mexico, some of the band gaily waved and stepped down from the train into their new assignments. This gave Daisy and Noley the opportunity to share closer quarters. Seattle and the South meshed like fine shears; Daisy preferred the upper bunk, Noley the lower. Whispered secrets far into the night brought them close as sisters and their shared faith added to the friendship.

Now they traveled almost due west. Terrain changed. The first glimpse of red buttes left the pair speechless and the dry-mud rivers with not much water in them beneath trestles raised their eyebrows. "It's not like this where we're going," Daisy comforted. "There are trees at Williams, lots of them." Yet the very next day those placid rivers changed their sleepy course. Rain poured onto the parched land and the water had no place to go because of the hard-caked ground. It ran in torrents into every dip and ravine and gully. Overnight, seeds the conductors said had lain dormant for years sprang into the tiniest of plants and the hot sun popped open flowers until they carpeted the desert. "Look while you can," a friendly conductor told his staring passengers. "You may never again see this happen. It takes the exact right conditions to make the posies bloom."

"It won't be long now," Noley whispered to Daisy that night. "I can hardly wait."

"Nor can I." Yet even after her friend's steady breathing showed she slept, Daisy lay wide-eyed. She couldn't decide if the strange desolation that had crept into her heart came from fear of what lay ahead or homesickness. She fell asleep to the tuneless rhythm of train wheels and dreamed they carried her farther and farther away from home, so far she could never return. Yet the smell of smoke from their great fireplace swirled around her and her nostrils flared from the scent. She struggled to open her heavy eyelids, trapped in the gray land between sleep and awareness. A mighty shudder went through the train. She dimly heard the scream of a monster that could not be held in check. The car lurched, tipped. Daisy instinctively clung to the sides of the berth. She felt a blow to her head, searing pain, then velvet blackness surrounded her.

"Daisy."

She fought the weakness that kept her from answering her mother's soft call. Driving her teeth into her lower lip, scarcely aware of what she did, she again forced her eyes open, to utter chaos. This time the smoke that stung her nose and throat were no imaginary dreamings, but real. Lurid light from leaping flames sent horror through her. Still dazed, Daisy realized she lay at an odd angle and knowledge that the passenger car must be on its right side slowly seeped into her brain. Else why would Noley's berth be above her? Why did a heavy weight press on her legs and body?

Noley! Memory sponged bewilderment effectively and she tried to free herself from the clutch of wreckage that pinned her down. "Noley?"

"Here." But the voice sounded faint and faraway.

"Are you hurt? Can you get out?"

"I'm all right and free, but I can't get you out. It's too heavy."

Daisy heard sobs and saw fresh fire spurt up, closer to them this time. She squirmed and broken window glass slid from her covers. Fear beyond anything she'd known surged through her, not for herself, but for the coura-

geous friend who still sobbed and attacked the impris-
oning debris. "Get out, Noley," she screamed. "Do you
hear me? Leave me here and go! See if you can find
help," she added, not because she expected it but to force
Noley to leave her. "You aren't strong enough and neither am I."

"Pray, Daisy." The other girl leaned over her, eyes
pools of dark terror.

"I will. Now, *go*." She saw Noley lurch away, heard
the crunch of glass beneath her feet. Then she lay alone,
waiting for the end. Her mother's words from weeks
ago returned to haunt her. *I can promise. . .if you continue to follow your own path. . .one day no one will be
there to help you.* She writhed with anguish and pain.
She had set her feet on this path and it had trapped her.
Must she die in this inferno when every nerve and muscle
shouted the desire to live? With all her ebbing strength
she tried to free herself. She failed.

"God, help Your child," she cried in a final attempt to
blot out the screams and groans in the distance. Seconds
ticked into minutes that felt like eons. Then a clear and
ringing voice spoke.

"Cover your face."

"God, is it You?" She automatically obeyed, heart
racing. Was her death to be so terrible her Heavenly
Father didn't want her to see the end?

"No." A mighty wrenching sound followed. Coughing, sputtering from the grey cloud of smoke, Daisy felt
a weight lift from her body. Hope flared, dimmed when
she tried to move. Her legs still lay pinned.

"Save yourself," she desperately said, but the only an-

swer she received came with heavy breathing from her
rescuer's heroic efforts and a fresh spell of coughing.
Daisy raised herself up and saw a tall man whose light
jacket strained with the task of lifting the weight from
her feet. Hair darkened with perspiration, face above a
bandana tied over his nose, and mouth ghastly in the
light, he ordered in a muffled, grunting voice, "When I
lift, slide back."

Her muscles ached in sympathy when he gave a mighty
tug but she jerked her bare feet upwards just in time.
She winced when something sharp tore into the flesh of
her leg but didn't cry out. The next moment, the stranger
dropped his burden. He snatched her from the berth into
his arms, flipped the blanket over her head, and started
down the aisle, only to stop. "Dear God, no!"

She knew it for a prayer and tore the blanket free. A
wall of flame faced them. He turned, awkward from her
weight. New fire had sprung up. Daisy felt the muscles
of his arms contract, then expand. "Only one way." He
set her on her feet, turned toward the broken window,
and groped for the blanket around her shoulders. In the
light of the fire, she saw him wrap it around his hands
and pound out the remaining jagged glass.

The next instant he crawled through and grunted,
"Don't be afraid. There's room to stand."

Somehow she managed to climb out of the hellish
scene, to breathe air a degree fresher than inside but still
smoke-laden. She peered down. Fresh horror consumed
her. Below them lay water, deep, dark, and menacing.
Daisy braced herself, knowing what he'd say.

"We have no choice. You must do exactly as I tell

you." He grabbed the blanket and discarded it, tore free his jacket. "There may be oil on the water. If so, it could ignite at any time. When we hit the water, *we must stay underneath* until I can get you away from danger. Can you swim at all?"

"Yes."

"We can't take a chance on being separated. Grab my belt on my left side. No matter what happens, don't let go. Kick with your feet, as hard as you can." He wasted no more time in explaining. "God willing, we'll make it." He placed her hands on his belt and whipped the bandana from his face.

Daisy strained to see but his broad shoulders blocked her view for he looked straight down. "Remember, hang on." He reached behind and grabbed her right wrist with his left hand in a grasp that hurt. "Now!" The next instant they fell through space and into unplumbed depths.

She had reason enough left to fill her tortured lungs with air the moment before the waters claimed them. Long before they finally surfaced, she felt she must gasp for air, even though doing so meant death by drowning. Yet even when she knew she could stand no more, her fingers locked on his belt and her feet continued to kick, although feebly. They shot up, up, until Daisy grew aware of cold air on her face in place of water. She gulped it in and her brain cleared. Her rescuer swam with long, sure strokes that conquered the river. Now she could help more. Daring to free her left hand from his life-sustaining belt, she fell into a kicking, stroking rhythm that matched his. She could hear his labored breathing. How long could he keep going? Surely God wouldn't allow them to escape the burning car to drown. Should she loosen her right hand's clutch and let him save himself?

As if he divined the thought he gasped, "Don't let go. Almost there." A minute or two more and they lay panting on the riverbank, safe from harm.

Moments or hours later, Daisy couldn't tell which, the stranger forced out, "Are you hurt?"

She started to tell him of her torn leg, the aching bump on her head, then felt ashamed. Compared with the magnificent fight he had just won, her injuries were nothing. "Mostly frightened and relieved." Her teeth chattered.

He stripped off his shirt. "It won't help much but here." He picked her up the way a child does a doll and carried her farther back from the riverbank. "Stay here. I'll send help."

"Oh, don't go!" The night's terrors transmitted themselves into fingers that clutched at his arm.

"I must. There are others." Before she could speak, he left her, chilled and pulling the wet shirt around her.

Reaction set in and the knowledge she couldn't stay here. The Arizona night felt strangely cold and great white stars shone down on her. She flayed herself for being a weakling and got to her feet. Above her, the derailed train with its burning cars held death. She had been saved, but what about Noley, their companions, the brave man who taried to pry her from her berth and risk his life? Even now, he might be up there searching the wreckage for those who needed him.

Daisy's fighting Irish spirit rose. No O'Rourke must snivel on a riverbank at such a time. She got to her feet, scrambled in the direction her rescuer had gone, and inch by inch gained higher ground. Low-growing bushes snatched at her bare feet and ankles. She heard tears and knew her nightgown had been rent by their reaching thorns. Her tender feet ached from sharp stones and stickers, but she continued. The long journey back became a challenge, something she had to do if ever she could live with herself again and not be ashamed.

She reached a huddled band of stranded travelers, some Harvey Girls. "Noley?" she demanded.

They turned to her as if she were a ghost. A slight, white-clad form rushed from their midst. Warm arms surrounded her. "Daisy, thank God! We thought you were dead." Noley's beautiful face contorted with shock and grief mingled with gladness. "I couldn't find anyone to help. They were all elsewhere. I tried to go back but sheets of flame swept between." The arms tightened. "I wished I'd stayed with you."

"I sent you away, remember?" Daisy pushed Noley away and looked from her to the others. "I don't understand. If you didn't send help, who did?" No one knew.

All during the rest of the horrendous night, that same unanswered question beat into Daisy's tired brain. Kindly ranchers nearby responded to word of the tragedy and opened their homes for the passengers until morning, when wagons and buggies and carriages quickly transported survivors to the nearest station down the line. The trestle required work and crews headed out at daybreak to clear the track and rebuild. A special train came out of the West, gathered up the shaken passengers, and sped back the way it came.

Daisy talked with every person she could contact in

an effort to learn her rescuer's identity. Her aching head and slight limp from the dressed leg wound didn't prevent her from pursuing what few leads she had. She reviewed them aloud for Noley.

"Tall, dark-looking hair but so sweaty it might be brown, not black. Strong or he couldn't have lifted as he did. A pleasant voice, one with authority." She sighed. "I know it sounds slight but I never actually saw his face."

"We'll find him," her friend comforted. "If only I'd seen him." She paused and her dark eyes widened. "Daisy, I don't know how he got to you. Which direction did he come from and when?"

"He just appeared, after I prayed." She felt the color drain from her face and clutched at Noley for support. "You don't thing I imagined him, do you? I couldn't have jumped in the river and swum to shore by myself."

"And angels don't wear sooty shirts twice as big as those you wear," Noley laughed. "He had to be real, but where is he?" She bit her lip and Daisy saw horror creep into her eyes. "He isn't among the dead."

"How do you know?"

She swallowed, started to speak, then paused and tried again. "I looked. I knew you had to find out. Only two men died and neither fit your description."

"You did that for me?" Daisy fought her feelings. If once they broke the dam inside her, she would never stop crying.

The horror faded and Noley's eyes looked normal again. "It seemed so little to do, after. . ." She couldn't continue. When she finally found her voice again she whispered, so low Daisy had to bend close to hear. "I'll always know God sent him to save you when I couldn't."

Daisy shivered, remembering the panic of being trapped, the fire, the plunge and moment in the river she knew she couldn't carry on. "I believe that, too. Oh, Noley." The dam burst with a mighty roar. "I didn't even thank him."

# eight

John Talbot left Illinois with hopes that soared even higher the farther west he traveled. His dark brown eyes opened wide at the strange country so different from the rolling, fertile land he left behind. The sight of his first jackrabbit brought a chuckle. Ridiculous looking beast, staring at the train, then bounding away on long legs that covered a lot of territory in every leap. John also stored up many memories he privately labeled *firsts*. First whiff of pungent sagebrush from the platform when the train halted in a small town. First sight of snow-capped mountains in the distance. First mile into New Mexico Territory, with his hand surreptitiously clutching the worn letter bearing a faded, beckoning postmark. He had thrilled when he located El Cinco, a tiny dot on the map north of Santa Fe on the eastern slopes of the Sangre de Cristo mountains. He knew from recent studies of the area the mountain's name meant "Blood of Christ." The hamlet lay miles from the railroad and John would leave the train at Springer, where the conductor assured him he could hire a horse or wait until a stage left.

"You don't happen to have heard of a Johnny Talbot, by any chance." His heartbeat quickened.

The conductor regretfully shook his grizzled head. "Naw, I don't know folks in these parts. You might say, I'm always just-a-passin' through." A wide grin at his own wit creased the man's face and John laughed appreciatively. He'd known the improbability of such a long chance paying off.

Neither did anyone he met in Springer seem to know anything about his father, although he talked with the postmaster, storekeeper, and livery stable owner.

El Cinco started out just as disappointing. John had chosen to buy a horse rather than hire one. Another horse on the ranch couldn't help but be welcome. Besides, who knew when or if he'd be back in Springer? Always methodical, he took a long time choosing, then at last selected a fine black named Crowfoot. "He has a habit of stepping sideways if'n you don't watch him," the seller warned. "Other than that, he's as fine a cayuse as you could throw a leg over." He named what John suspected was an exorbitant price and the canny Easterner laughed outright.

"I may be an Illinois farm boy but I know horseflesh. I'll give you half of that."

A lot of bluster and headshaking later, John settled for a figure in between and rode away satisfied at both his new mount and the rueful grin on the livery stable owner's face. He purchased a used but excellent saddle, tack and enough food for the sunup to sundown trip the horse trader said he'd need to ride to El Cinco. "What does it mean?" he'd asked, amused at the odd name.

"Five, I reckon. That's Mex."

"Five rivers? Five mountains?"

"Who cares? A name's a name, ain't it?" The man looked astonished.

John barely held in his laughter and once out of earshot with Springer behind him, let out the "yippy-ki-yi" cowboy's yell he'd heard from the train when a fun-loving group of riders chased it out of a dusty town, to the entertainment of the passengers. Crowfoot snorted and glanced back long enough to look his new rider over, then went into his two-step routine. John pressed with his knees, reined him in, and the black settled into a mile-devouring and surprisingly comfortable pace.

Darkness encroached on the foothills by the time they reached El Cinco and shadows lay like mighty fingers of a giant hand. Unused to such long hours on horseback, John slid from the saddle and limped his way to the livery stable at the end of the single, wide street. He personally rubbed Crowfoot down, learned that the Grubstake had the best food in town—for that matter, the only food, since "'tis our only cafe" the laconic stableman drawled—and that "Miz Carrington's" rooming house had a vacancy.

"Do you know a Johnny Talbot?" the newcomer asked.

"Who wants to know?"

The sharp question set a warning bell clanging at the crossroads of John's mind. "A—friend. My name's John Ashley." Flabbergasted at leaving off his last name, he recovered when the other man said, "Did he have a small spread near here?"

"I believe so." That same warning bell made John cautious.

"He ain't here now."

"Where'd he go? Why?"

In the dimness of the stable the air hung with unspoken words before the reply came. "I got nothin' more to say."

John knew further questioning would avail nothing, but couldn't resist a parting shot. "Who would?"

"Might try the sheriff, young feller. Hope you find El Cinco to your likin'."

What a strange encounter! The searcher felt torn between dismay and fear counter balanced with hope. At least Dad had been here, talked with the livery stable owner, in all probability eaten at the Grubstake, perhaps stayed at "Miz Carrington's". A feeling of closeness hovered, then reluctantly withdrew. What had happened to keep the man from talking?

John headed for the rooming house first, got installed in a sparsely furnished but spotless upstairs bedroom, and amiably agreed the hour was certainly too late to expect a body to answer questions about things that didn't concern her. His new and billowy landlady's remark added to his suspicion and again he simply gave his name as John Ashley. He bathed, shook the dust from his clothes before again donning them, and grimaced. Why hadn't he thought to stuff a clean outfit in his saddlebags? The erratic stage service from Springer to El Cinco meant a day or two wait before his trunk arrived. He'd made arrangements before leaving the larger town but had been too impatient to get going to think of taking extra clothing.

"If the stage doesn't get here tomorrow, I'll buy a few new clothes," he soliloquized and headed in search of supper.

Curious stares and a hush in the chatter of roughly garbed men greeted him when he stepped inside the

Grubstake. For a few moments he felt much the way a stranger in town in the wilder and woollier days must have done. "Howdy," he told the man behind a long counter. "I hear your place has the best food in town." He smiled.

Loud haw-haws greeted his sally and the proprietor couldn't hide a grin. "What you want, cowboy?"

"Steak. Fried potatoes. Green stuff, if you have it." Since he'd been taken for a cowpuncher, John decided to make the most of it. A known tenderfoot would have even more trouble getting to the bottom of a mystery, if there were one, than a newcomer. "Apple pie? Sure. Black coffee, too."

"You just passing through?" the friendly cafe owner busied himself with gleaming spatula on a grill just behind him.

"Maybe. I rode in from Springer." John let out a sigh of appreciation when what he believed had to be the world's biggest steak came on a platter just smaller than some of the ponds back home. A mountain of fried potatoes snuggled up against the steak and various side dishes made his mouth water.

"If you need work, I hear some of the ranchers are looking for hands for fall roundup. That is, if you aim to stay that long." An oblique glance betrayed curiosity.

John appreciatively took a bite of steak. "Which one serves the best grub?" He cut off another juicy hunk.

"Say, you're all right." The acceptance started the buzz of voices that had remained still until John more or less identified himself and again, he wondered. Bite by bite he stuffed himself, topping off with pie and more coffee, gleaning bits of information from the talk around him. A few casually worded questions elicited the information many of the smaller ranches were being taken over by a syndicate but folks didn't seem to know the man behind it.

"Who are some of those who got ousted?" John asked in a mildly interested way. Meaningless names followed then a voice said from behind him, "Don't forget Johnny Talbot." It took every ounce of self-control John possessed to keep from whipping around. Instead he took another swallow of coffee.

"Reckon honest folks around here won't forget Talbot," the Grubstake owner said significantly.

"Who is this Talbot?" John innocently inquired.

"Just a guy who got a raw deal."

"I'll say he did—" But the unidentified speaker broke off when someone else put in, "He couldn't prove it so why gab about it? Say, Hall, what'll you take for that little pinto of yours?" Good-natured wrangling followed and John waited a reasonable length of time, then stood, praised his meal again, and strode out after nodding to the cafe's patrons.

"Who is that jasper, anyway?" he heard someone idly say.

"Just a puncher like the rest of you yahoos, drifting and not much interested in anything 'cept a good meal and a good hoss," another pegged him.

John grinned in the darkness and started for Miz Carrington's and a good night's sleep.

A day of sauntering from the post office housed in the corner of a mercantile to the stage stop when the coach rolled in added tiny pieces of hard-won information to the puzzle of Johnny Talbot. He hadn't reckoned on the deadly accuracy of small town gossip, however. When he went back to the Grubstake for supper, the proprietor eyed him and bluntly demanded.

"How come you're so interested in Johnny Talbot? I heard you've been asking about him all over town." He sounded upset.

John made a quicksilver decision. "I used to know him, a long time ago when I was just a kid. About a year ago he wrote to a friend of mine saying he'd had good luck and owned a ranch near here. After my folks died I decided to come here; thought he might give me a job riding."

"Why didn't you say so last night?" Suspicion shone bright in the watching gaze.

John realized he was on trial from the way the cafe grew quiet. He grinned his disarming grin. "I figured I'd learn more if I kept mum and listened. You know the good Lord gave us two ears and one mouth 'cause He expects us to do twice as much listening as talking."

Laughter erupted, but John mentally gave thanks for his narrow escape. When the room quieted, he turned toward a small table surrounded by riders. "I'd sure appreciate it if you could give me some clue to what happened, why and where Talbot went."

Faces closed like shutters against a cold night, all but one frank-faced puncher who drawled, "Stranger, it's the old story. Big fish gobbles down little fish. One week Talbot had this purty spread. The next week, the syndicate claims it's theirs—and proves it in court, all legal-like; their fancy lawyer had deeds and stuff to show. All Talbot had was a bill of sale from the feller he bought the ranch from."

"But didn't he swear the sale was legal?"

Meaningful looks passed between the men. "Naw. He up and vamoosed before the hearing. Nobody's seen or heard of him since." A long pause followed, then the young rider added in a deadly tone. "Talbot hung around for a time, then got wind of something, didn't say what. He saddled up and rode out. Word came back he'd been seen in Albuquerque, then Gallup. 'Pears he headed west, probably into Arizona, tracking the varmint what cheated him."

"Did the varmint have a name?" John's lips thinned.

"Yup, at least on the bill of sale. Dan Smith."

"What did he look like?"

Regret filled the loquacious puncher's face and he shook his head. "No one in El Cinco ever saw him, leastways, not as Dan Smith."

"So the only one who can identify the cheat is Talbot."

"Uh-huh. 'Course, *some folks*—" His pause underlined the words. "Some couldn't help wondering if the syndicate, whoever they are, knew anything about it, but a feller can find it unhealthy, sticking his nose in other people's business. Besides, the way I hear tell, Talbot did everything he could to prove his claim. Nobody else could do more."

"So you think he was robbed?"

The cowboy's steady gaze never wavered, even when he quietly replied, "Now, what's a poor, lonesome cowpoke know? He just rides the range, sings his little dogies to sleep, and minds his own affairs—'specially when he's saving enough to get hitched." Silence settled over the room. His voice lowered and he went on, "I s'pose some might feel a man and a town should take it on themselves to interfere but I reckon those are the kind of folks who didn't do what they could before riding plumb into a wall."

John knew what he needed to know. His smile thanked the talkative cowboy but he chose his words carefully. "For what it's worth from a man just riding through, El Cinco is home to a lot of fine people."

"You're going to be moseying on?" the proprietor asked.

"Yes. For some reason, I have a hankering to see some more of New Mexico Territory, maybe even Arizona."

Understanding gleamed in the helpful rider's eyes and he nodded. "Good luck. Say, what did you say your name was? If Talbot shows up back here, we'll tell him you're heading west."

Emotion threatened to close John's throat. "Just tell him John Ashley hoped to find him." Before he could betray that far more than friendship lay in the search, he left, but hesitated on the porch and heard someone demand,

"Why'd you go and spill the beans?"

The clear voice of the cowpuncher reached John. "Aw, somehow I felt like he needed to know. At least I didn't tell him that Talbot raved and said when he caught up with his man, there's be one less Dan Smith in New Mexico Territory."

Sick at heart, wet with cold sweat, John noiselessly got away. Now more than ever he must find his father before Johnny Talbot took revenge on his enemy in a fight that could only end with spilled blood.

By daybreak the next morning, John had his plans made. He interviewed Miz Carrington, generously rewarded her for the trouble it would take in seeing his trunk got picked up and shipped to Gallup, the last known stop in Johnny's pursuit. He routed out the livery stable owner, saddled Crowfoot, and headed down the tumbleweed trail, driven by the devils of worry and fear. Mile after fretful mile gave way to the black's steady, almost tireless pace. Each time the wanderers met up with rider, traveler or townsperson, John asked about two men: Johnny Talbot and Dan Smith. He continued to go by the name John Ashley, an instinctive protection against lips that would remain closed to John Talbot, son.

Sante Fe proved picturesque and would have held his interest at any other time. Albuquerque offered no clues to the disappearance of his father. At Gallup, a saloon-keeper claimed to vaguely remember someone named Talbot who had come and gone months earlier but admitted no face came to mind. When questioned further, he thought maybe the man had been headed for Arizona Territory but couldn't say for sure and had no idea where in Arizona. John sighed, got what he could carry from his trunk, and gave the rest to the man.

A succession of disappointments followed. Every lead ended in the blank wall the cowpuncher in El Cinco had mentioned. If Johnny Talbot had actually gone to

Arizona Territory, it must have swallowed him without a trace, the way mystery herds of cattle vanished, hide, hooves and tail into secret draws, never to reappear.

Footsore and weary, John plodded on. He grew thinner but harder even than he'd been from his farm work. Crowfoot kept him company and the feeling God saw and understood his quest brought comfort. A hundred time he prayed, "Lord, help me find Dad before he does something terrible." It became a talisman, a petition constantly in his heart.

After scouring the eastern part of Arizona Territory, he headed north and west, following the railroad line, asking at every town, village, and inhabited shack along the way. At Holbrook, the ticketmaster swore he remembered a John Talbot, because of the flinty look in his eyes when he bought a ticket to Flagstaff and a broken comment, "Now I'll find him and when I do—" It had impressed the man who repeated it.

With the lightning decision-making process John had learned on his long journey, plus an inner compulsion to get to his father as quickly as possible, he put Crowfoot into the care of the Holbrook livery stable and boarded the train, promising to return soon. He had no idea how soon it would be.

Dozing in his seat, mind racing ahead, John came wide awake from a grinding shudder so violent it threw him forward. His head struck the frame of the seat ahead and he slumped to the heaving floor of the coach. Semiconscious, he tried to rouse but the effort seemed too much and he lay where he'd fallen; how long, he had no way of knowing, vaguely conscious of darkness and screaming, then leaping light and the acrid smell of smoke.

Ironically, the bitter smell cleared his brain. He straightened, touched a lump that had risen on his head, and heaved a sigh of relief when his hand remained dry. Evidently the blow hadn't broken the skin.

Now the flames inched closer, while screams sounded more distant. He leaped to his feet, crawled over wreckage, and discovered no passengers remained in the coach. Huddled between the seats in the darkness, he had been overlooked. Little time remained before the entire coach became an inferno. John reached the door at the end of the car, opened it, and stepped out. Blessed relief from the cold night air sent thankfulness through him. He filled his lungs, uttered a quick prayer, and wrenched open the door of the sleeping car next to the coach after realizing no path of escape lay beneath him, only vast darkness intermittently revealed as a pile of rocks by vagrant flames.

He passed through the car, rejoicing to find it empty. When he entered the next, he caught a dim glimpse of a woman's skirt disappearing out the other door; the echo of a voice pleading, "Help, someone. She's—" The closing door shut off the words and generated horror. Through thickening smoke he groped, aided only by touch and the handkerchief he'd bound around nose and mouth, until he heard a low voice in prayer.

"God, help Your child." It hung in the smoky gloom.

John fought his way down the side-turned sleeping car, hampered by its unnatural position, clinging to the side of the berths until a spurt of fire revealed a dark huddle

in what had once been an upper berth. Thank God! More
flames gave light enough to see the weight pinning the
hapless passenger down. "Cover your face," he ordered.

"God, is it You?"

"No." He wrenched a great piece of debris away and
a girl's voice pleaded, "Save yourself," but John didn't
even hesitate. With strength born of desperation, he
worked until he could gather her in his arms. "Dear
God, no!"

A wall of flame faced them.

A quick survey of the luridly lit coach showed their
only way of escape and it guaranteed nothing. Knowing
the fire gave no quarter, he smashed the remaining glass
in the window, crawled out and lifted the girl he couldn't
see through. A quick plunge, icy water, long, swift
strokes in a river bent on claiming its victims left him
feeling they'd been in its depths forever. The moment
came when he knew that even with the feeble one-armed
movement and kicking by his burden they couldn't make
it. A silent prayer flung itself to the star-studded sky. A
minute later, he saw they had nearly reached the shore.
His feet touched bottom and with the girl's hand still
clutching his belt, John staggered from the greedy water.

A brief exchange of words, the realization others like
her might still be saved, and he left her, feeling he'd
deserted. He started away, intending to climb to high
ground but the strain he'd been under proved too much.
Instead of turning right toward the wreck, he turned left,
directly toward the sound of rushing hooves and the clat-
ter of a wagon. His tongue felt thick when he tried to

tell the men who sprang to his side the spunkiest girl he'd ever known lay waiting for help on the riverbank. John felt himself lifted and wrapped in something soft and warm. Gradually his chattering teeth stilled. He tried to remember what it was he should do. Oh, yes, he must get Crowfoot and go on with his journey. Dad needed him "Holbrook," he muttered, then slid into the sleep his overtaxed body and mind cried out for.

## nine

A subdued group of Harvey Girls joined the other westbound passengers at the next station on the line the day after the wreck. "We can never thank you enough," Noley told the warmhearted rancher and his wife who had taken her and Daisy in, along with several others.

"Sho, you're the ones who should be thanked," their host blustered, eyes Arizona-sky blue in his weather-beaten face. "We must seem mighty rough out here an' we plumb appreciate you gals who're willin' to come help us make this here Territory fit for somethin' other than rattlesnakes and buzzards—although we've got them, and they don't all crawl or fly. Keep your eyes out for two-legged varmints."

Daisy opened her mouth to tell him Arizona couldn't be any wilder than Washington when her folks went there, then clamped her lips shut. One of these times she'd let slip that she wasn't a proper Kansas lady but if she could keep her secret until after proving herself, maybe it wouldn't be so important.

A cautious inquiry of those who had been in the accident still failed to turn up any information about the mysterious rescuer who had—as Noley said—"come out of the west like young Lochinvar" in Sir Walter Scott's famous poem. Miss Magnolia Symington had almost completely recovered her composure. Now her black-pansy eyes flashed with fun and she giggled. "We don't know that, of course."

"Know what?" Daisy felt dull and slow-witted compared with her new friend.

"Know that he came out of the West. Maybe he's an Easterner." She clasped her hands and looked soulful. "It's so romantic."

"Romantic!" Daisy remembered the awful flames, the long plunge, the icy water, and shuddered.

"Oh, I don't mean the wreck. Just that when you needed help most, God sent the stranger. What kind of clothes did he have on?"

"I remember a light-colored jacket, casual," Daisy slowly replied. "A bandana, that covered his face until just before we jumped." She shook her head. "He didn't look Eastern."

"How about his voice? Would you know it again?"

"I don't know." Feeling suddenly tired, she closed her eyes and leaned her head back against the plush seat back. "We know he isn't dead but that doesn't mean I-we'll ever see him again. Noley, I don't want to talk about it now."

"I understand." A quick pressure of the Southern girl's hand conveyed sympathy and Daisy soon fell into an exhausted sleep. She awakened to the bustle and hum of voices she knew signified a train stop just ahead.

"Flagstaff! All off for Flagstaff." The conductor trumpeted his way down the aisle and disappeared into the next car.

Daisy couldn't believe she had slept all those miles. A sleepy-eyed Noley yawned and sat bolt upright.

"Flagstaff?" She squeezed Daisy's arm. "Williams is less than thirty miles from here." Fright crept into her voice. "What if we aren't any good? I can't bear it if they send me home."

The anguish in her voice set Daisy's heart thumping. "Now's a fine time to think such a thing. Of course we'll make good. Think I'm going to miss my big chance after all I went through to get here? Mercy, no. If I can learn to be Miss Templeton, live through a train wreck, a miraculous rescue, and an unwelcome swim in a flooded river, I can be the Harvey-est Girl ever you saw and so can you, Magnolia."

Color crept back into Noley's strained face. So did the mischief that changed her from attractive to startlingly beautiful. "Then so can I."

"Arizona sure isn't like where I come from." Daisy pressed her nose to the window but growing darkness dimmed edges and she couldn't see much beyond the tracks.

A small voice, echoed, "Not like the South either. Dear me, I hope I won't be homesick." The plaintive note whipped Daisy around.

"Don't you dare be," she fiercely ordered. "If you are, I will be too, and it will spoil everything. If you start thinking about plantations and cotton fields and magnolias, remember all the cowboys and ranchers who are just waiting for you to come."

Noley's clear, ringing laugh dispelled the languid scene in favor of the more active one. "I'm so glad we'll be here together."

"So am I." The closer they came to Williams, the

more fervently Daisy felt that way. The excitement of going, urged on by Daphne, the trip itself, even the wreck had stimulated her. Now she thanked God another girl just as unfamiliar with the West would be entering her new life with her.

Neither of them ever forgot the first evening in Williams. Although Williams had boasted a Harvey House eating establishment since 1887, the Fray Marcos Hotel had just opened. Because of the close proximity to the south rim of the Grand Canyon of the Colorado River, farseeing Fred Harvey and his associates captured both those traveling East and West plus visitors to the Canyon; some chose to stay before journeying the final sixty miles to one of the seven wonders of the world.

At their request, the friends were allowed to room together in a beautiful, well-kept room. The house mother, whom they knew also served as chaperone, took one look at the weary girls and quietly said, "Time enough tomorrow for you to get uniforms and learn the house rules. You two look as if a good night's sleep will do wonders." She showed them the bathing accommodations, spotless and shining.

"We don't have nightgowns," Daisy faltered, perilously close to tears at the motherly woman's kindness, although she suspected it would be woe unto any young woman in her charge who broke a rule. "We lost everything in the wreck."

"Oh, didn't they tell you?" Mrs. Hill looked astonished. "The baggage car escaped the flames so except for what you carried with you and lost, everything is intact. You did have other sleeping garments, didn't you?"

"Oh, yes," Noley breathed. "Thank God our clothes didn't get burned." She blushed. "I don't mean to sound selfish. It's just that—"

"I understand." Her mild blue eyes showed sympathy and her light brown bun bobbed when she nodded. Rounder than either girl and between them in height, her cotton dress crackled with starch. She pointed to the trunks set in an obscure corner. "By the time you bathe and get ready for bed I'll have a tray waiting, just for this time. Goodnight, girls. I hope you'll be happy here."

"We will," Daisy immediately told her. Sight of the room and the woman's friendliness had unknotted her nerves.

An hour later Noley groaned and admitted, "If this is a sample of Fred Harvey food, no wonder people rush to eat in Harvey Houses."

"I agree." Daisy ruefully looked at the remains of a small roasted chicken, mashed potatoes and stuffing, three kinds of vegetables, a lone ripe red tomato slice on a bit of lettuce and the well-scraped crystal goblets that had held the most delicious whipped pudding she'd ever eaten. "If this is supposed to be a 'tray' just think of what's in store for us tomorrow."

"Do I have to?" Noley left the small table and flopped on the bed. "I'll look like a cotton puff on sticks if I eat like this." She stretched luxuriantly.

"I imagine by the time we put in the long hours our job requires, we won't have to worry about getting fat," Daisy reflected. She set the demolished dinner tray outside their door, hastily cleaned her teeth, and tumbled into bed. No nightmares of wrecks tonight, just deep and dreamless sleep. She awakened to brilliant sunshine when Noley caroled, "Wake up, sleepyhead. Today we become Harvey Girls." She giggled irrepressibly. "I'll wager you just can't wait to get into one of those penguin uniforms."

"They aren't so bad," Daisy said later, when clad in the regulation clothing some said Fred Harvey had personally chosen to blunt public criticism of young women away from home. First introduced in 1883, its nun-like appearance consisted of a plain black skirt scrupulously shortened or lengthened to exactly eight inches from the floor, high collared black shirt, white bib and apron, black shoes, stockings, and hairnet. The two newcomers actually looked rather fetching in the stark simplicity that set off Daisy's copper hair and Noley's white skin.

"Good thing we don't use cosmetics," Noley whispered. "I heard that the management in some places actually took a wet cloth to the girls' faces to make sure they weren't wearing paint of any kind." She bit her lips to redden them—and learned a lesson when Mrs. Hill inspected her new charges.

"Miss Symington, is that lip rouge?" she demanded sternly.

"No, ma'am." Her face turned peony red. "I bit my lips to make them red."

"And succeeded admirably," their housemother snapped, even though her blue eyes twinkled. "I suggest you do nothing to give the appearance of rule breaking from now on."

"I won't."

*Neither will I,* Daisy vowed. Kind and understanding Mrs. Hill might be, but she obviously would tolerate no infractions of her rules.

"If you spill anything, no matter how small an amount, you are to immediately change to a clean uniform," Mrs. Hill instructed. "You will be issued enough sets to allow for this. Now, about your schedules. You will work six-day weeks, twelve hours a day but shifts are split to accommodate the meal trains. While not actually engaged in serving, silver always needs polishing and work stations must be kept spotless."

Daisy felt a flutter in her throat. "Miss Hill, we're both Christians." Her voice sounded thin and reedy in her ears. "Is there any way we could have Sundays off? I mean, we'd like to attend church," she ended breathlessly, fingers clenched and hidden by the fullness of her starched apron.

Mrs. Hill cocked her head to one side and silently surveyed them. "We like our girls to be good influences in our communities," she said after a moment. "If I can arrange it, yes, but it depends on how many of the other waitresses also want Sunday off. I'm inclined to grant your request over those who simply wish time for their own pursuits, but I'm also afraid it can't be every week."

"Thank you," they chorused and Daisy relaxed her sweaty palms.

The end of their first meal of actual serving left them limp. Despite the excellent training they'd been given, serving a horde of harried, hurried travelers—all of whom were not sweetness and light—proved a far different situation than during practice. The end of their first full day saw them soaking in hot tubs, little caring if they lived or died.

"I can't imagine why some folks think Harvey Girls are wild." Noley rolled her black eyes. "Who has time to even think wild thoughts, let alone do bad things?"

"*I* can't imagine why I ever thought this would be a good way to see the West; to ride and visit ranches and all that," Daisy retorted. Then she laughed. "We see cowboys and ranchers, hundreds and thousands and millions of them—"

"Don't exaggerate," came from the prone figure on the other bed.

"Well, what seems like hundreds and thousands and millions. But who has time to talk with any of them?"

"Daisy, do you believe in love at first sight? I mean, the Romeo and Juliet kind of love where you know he's the one?"

Weariness forgotten, Daisy shot upright. "You're the Southern belle. I don't know anything about real love except what's in the books." Suspicion began, grew. "Magnolia Symington, have you gone and fallen in love the first week we're here?" Her voice squeaked.

Noley sat up, face pink and black curls tumbled. "I don't know. That's why I asked you." Her eyes looked more like black pansies than ever. "All the boys and men back home bored me, they were all so the same; like our cook Dicey had stamped them out of biscuit dough and baked them to a nice brown doneness."

"But, who—is it Tom?" Intense concentration brought to mind the hale and hearty, ruddy-faced rancher who had sat at Noley's table a few hours earlier. Thirty or so, Tom Carew owned a nearby ranch and although too busy to pay much attention at the time, now Daisy remembered the smitten way he'd stared at her friend and how she plotted to tease later.

"Yes." She looked small, huddled on the other bed. "He left me *five dollars* for a tip and when he finished eating he told the men with him he reckoned it wouldn't be long before someone dropped a halter on him. Do you think he meant me?"

"Don't be a goose. Who else could he mean?" The same pang that had touched Daisy at her cousin Daphne's wedding returned and flicked at her heart. Noley looked absolutely smitten. Disappointment crowded her throat. "You aren't going to break your contact, are you?"

The dark eyes opened wide. "Of course not. He may not even care and even if he does, then he can wait for me. It won't hurt him." A little smile curved her lips. "All the time I wanted to marry a cowboy, why, I thought it was just a dream. If Tom c-cares—" Her voice broke. "Will I make a good rancher's wife?" She brushed damp lashes with her fingers.

"You will make the best rancher's wife in Arizona," Daisy solemnly assured her friend, even though envy diluted her honest joy at Noley's happiness. "Do you really, truly believe Tom is the man God knows can bring you happiness?"

"I think so. Only it's more like he's the one I can make happy. Goodnight, dear, dear Daisy. I'll pray for you to meet someone as wonderful as Tom and. . ." Sleep robbed her of the rest of the sentence but Daisy remained awake in spite of her fatigue and wondered about many things.

Gradually, the work grew easier and the girls more competent. Daisy watched Noley open from bud to full flower, more beautiful than the blossom that lent her its name. Tom Carew rode in from his ranch each late afternoon, regardless of the weather. When autumn laid its yellow and gold hand on birch, alder, and cottonwood, turning the world to continual sunshine, he came, and the girls finally got to see the surrounding countryside, which they loved. When winter sent exploring fingers, retreated and returned, Tom appeared in a sleigh and with Mrs. Hill's permission, took Noley and several of the other girls riding. He came to the parlor set aside for such visits and sat with his back to the chattering young women whose sallies bounced off his broad shoulders while setting his sweetheart's cheeks on fire.

At Christmastime, a small, velvet box held a diamond solitaire and a shining-eyed Noley proudly displayed it, then put it away except for when she was off duty, in accordance with the Harvey tradition that allowed no jewelry while serving. Yet she staunchly refused to forget Daisy because of her new love. They spent what time together they could eke out between work and the tiny Southerner's hours with her fiancé.

The long hours and busy schedule had tramped down all but a few seeds of homesickness but at Christmas Daisy found it almost impossible to keep from recklessly breaking her contract and rushing home. Just thinking about the holiday gave her goose bumps of loneliness. The festivities around her did help some and the advent of two customers gave her food for thought. At first she paid little heed to either, although both certainly commanded attention but in different ways. One, whose name she didn't know, merely smiled, nodded rather than speaking other than to place his order, and hid his thoughts and feelings behind a lean, tanned face. Always pleasant, he never made calf-eyes at her the way some other riders did; neither did he attempt to carry on a flirtation with any of the other Harvey Girls.

"Probably married," one observed in a woman's chat one evening in the parlor when swirling snow kept even the most intrepid visitor—including Tom Carew—from appearing.

"He doesn't act married," another protested. "He's probably a woman hater." The speaker, a pert blonde, grinned broadly. "Believe me, if I can't get them to talk, they have to be woman-haters." Laughter followed, then the first speaker added,

"Daisy, why don't you get him to talk? He comes to your table oftener than to any of ours." Before she could answer a mocking voice put in, "So does Rex Winningham and he sure isn't a woman-hater."

"He must be forty," Noley said disdainfully. "Too old for Daisy." Her loyal glance and smile showed the dislike she had confessed to her friend concerning the owner of one of the biggest ranches near Williams, the RW. "Don't ask me why but I don't trust him." She wrinkled her nose and Daisy listened carefully. In the months that had made them inseparable, she'd learned what a shrewd, intelligent brain lived in the little brunette's head and respected her evaluation.

"Not for me." The blond stretched and grinned again.

"He's just the kind of catch I'm fishing for: big ranch, good looking, lots of money. I'm serving notice, girls, he's mine if I can get him, so hands off. That means you, too, Daisy."

She raised one silky eyebrow and shrugged. "You're welcome to him. I wouldn't have Rex Winningham if you served him up on one of those silver platters we have to polish all the time." The moment she made the statement she regretted it. "I'm sorry. That isn't a nice thing to say about anyone. It's just that I'm not interested." She didn't add that like Noley, she neither trusted the blunt rancher nor his sly compliments the other girls hadn't overheard.

A few days later she regretted her impulsive statement even more. She never discovered who carried tales, but someone thought her comment too good to keep from repeating. Or perhaps Winningham listened in on gossiping girls. In any event, he remained at a table in her area long after everyone else had gone, easily saying, "Run along, men. I'm going to have me another cup of coffee and talk to Miss Templeton here."

She longed to freeze him with a glance but refrained. Harvey Girls were to be courteous at all times. She began to move away and the bulky rancher, who carried his weight well and always made Daisy compare him with one of the tawny cougars back in Washington, lightly caught her wrist.

"Please let go, Mr. Winningham." She tugged to free herself but his large hand closed more tightly.

"Not until you explain what you meant about not having me even served up on a silver platter."

She felt herself go scarlet, then pale. "I shouldn't have said such an unkind thing. I apologize."

"I'm crazy about you, don't you know that?" he attempted to draw her closer. "If you aren't interested in a man who can give you anything you want, why'd you come out here, anyway?" His eyes looked more catlike than ever, half-closed and dangerous. "Isn't that what you women are all about, wanting to find husbands?" Still holding her wrist, he stood and pulled her close.

"Miss Templeton, is this man annoying you?" Mrs. Hill had appeared, seemingly from nowhere. "Mr. Winningham, I must ask you to release this young lady at once."

He dropped her hand and Daisy rubbed the red mark his fingers had created. "He is just going." Her voice shook in spite of herself.

To her amazement, the unpredictable rancher turned to the housemother. "I beg your pardon, and Miss Templeton's. I fear I let my admiration for her get ahead of my manners." He threw money to the table in the charged atmosphere. "Forgive me, please." Yet the shine in his eyes betrayed how little regret he felt. Under the disguise of stooping as if to pick up something from the floor he whispered for Daisy's ears alone, "I'll see you later," then left her with Mrs. Hill, whose formidable presence even a Rex Winningham could not long ignore.

# ten

Strong currents carried John in their depths. He fought his way up, up, toward the dim light above him. "Have to make it. Can't drown," he mumbled.

"No one ever drowned from a face washing, cowboy." A crisp voice drove back the waves, even as God once parted the Red Sea to save His children.

John opened his eyes and blinked. A rugged-faced woman bent above him, wet towel in her hand. "Where—?"

"You're in the doctor's office at Holbrook," the motherly woman told him. Her steady gray eyes held compassion and a smile. "You got quite a knock in the head, the way I hear it."

Memory returned in a mighty rush. John struggled to sit up but his nurse restrained him. He tore free. "I have to go. The girl. I left her on the riverbank. She's wet and cold an—"

"Stop fretting. You muttered all the way in from the train wreck. Soon as the boys left you, they high-tailed it back. By now the girl's been found and taken care of. You were talking so wild when you stumbled out in front of the wagon, they figured they'd best get you to a doctor and not wait to see about anyone else."

"How long have I been here?" John turned his head and looked out a shining clean window. "Have they

130

brought others in? Was anyone killed?" The idea seemed
grotesque in this sunny room.

"I can tell you're feeling better," she joshed and
crinkles appeared at the corners of her eyes. "It's God's
own mercy a lot more weren't killed than just two men,
bad as that is. A few others got cuts and burns but land
sakes, the ranchers' wives around here are used to patch-
ing up their menfolk so they could take care of the passengers, who are long since gone on the special train
they sent back from the next station. You were hauled in
late last night and it's 'most sundown. Doc says to keep
you one more night."

When mutiny turned John's mouth down she added,
"No need arguing. What Doc says goes."

"When will I see him?" John meekly asked.

"After I fetch you some grub and you eat every bite of
it." Her starched skirt swished when she walked toward
the door. "Wherever you're going will still be there tomorrow." The door opened and closed behind her and
John ruefully had to admit the idea of food took prece-
dence over any desire to sneak out before it came.

He relaxed as much as possible on the hard cot and
surveyed the white washed walls, free of adornment; the
peg on which his now dry and pressed clothing hung.
An exploratory finger touched his head and he felt relieved the swelling had gone down. What a little thing
to kick up a fuss after all he'd gone through the night
before! Shame filled him. Yet when he haltingly tried to
tell the tired-looking doctor how he felt, the good man
snapped him up short.

"Bodies and minds are curious things, son. So long as

there's something we have to do they'll keep going but once danger's gone by, they stand up and yell for rest. According to what we could piece out from your broken sentences, you lifted heavy wreckage, freed a young lady, then leaped into a river, fought it until you won, and saved both your lives."

"I planned to go back and help others." John nervously twitched the coarse blanket covering him.

"No need. Others did that." The doctor's heavy black brows met in the middle when he frowned. "What's this about you wanting to leave? Better stay tonight. I'll examine you first thing in the morning, if you like. You can probably go then."

"Thanks, doctor. I can pay you."

"Good." A smile crossed the craggy face. "There's those who can't, but I still treat them." He hastily strode to the door and banged through it.

"Why don't I feel that sense of urgency that made me leave Crowfoot and catch the train?" John pondered aloud. "God, I thought it was because of Dad." The blood rushed to his face. "Did *You* send the feeling, because the girl needed me? No one else could have reached her in time." For a long time he lay on his narrow cot giving thanks that whatever the reason, he'd been given the opportunity and strength to save a human life. Would he ever see the young woman again? Would he even recognize her except for her voice? John closed his eyes and tried to recall details. Slowly an image floated into his mind. Flames dancing on eyes that looked black with fear. Disheveled hair, reddish—or had that been a reflection of the fire? Not heavy, neither feather-light when he had snatched her from the berth.

He gave up. "I think I'll know her voice if I do meet her again," he said drowsily, then fell asleep thinking about the next day.

A clean bill of health, fervent thanks to the doctor and his nurse, a trip to the livery stable for Crowfoot, and John Ashley Talbot resumed his journey west. The ride to Flagstaff, nearly one hundred miles, offered a variety of different scenery: desert and plateau; shifting vari-colored sands; odd-looking bluffs horizontally striped with cream and rose and pink; distant mountains, valley and stream. No longer impelled by the growing urgency, John allowed Crowfoot to choose a comfortable pace and enjoyed the ride. He learned to travel from daybreak until the merciless sun made it unbearable for man or beast, then seek what shade he could find, drowse away the simmering afternoon hours and start again in the cool evening. Once he reached the tree-greened areas he felt relieved and reached Flagstaff with renewed hope.

Contrary to the earlier part of his search, inquiry at the biggest mercantile in town bore fruit, although bitter. "Johnny Talbot? Sure, he's here."

"Where will I find him?"

"More'n' likely at the Frontier." The merchant grinned.

"Is that a boarding house?"

"Naw, it's a saloon. Whatcha want Talbot for, anyhow?"

John pretended not to hear the ribald question and didn't answer. Disappointment like thick dust choked him. Dad, a saloon habitue? It couldn't be true. Yet his steps lagged as he slowly led Crowfoot down the wide street in the direction indicated by the merchant's crooked thumb. He hitched the black to the rail in front, took one step toward the raised board walk, and froze.

"Get out and stay out, you worthless bum!" The scuffle of feet and ringing denunciation were followed by the appearance of a frontier Goliath shoving a tall but lighter man in front of him out the opened doors. "Don't come back 'til you can pay yore debts like a man," the giant roared. With a mighty fling, he threw his prisoner into the street, to the obvious enjoyment of the group of hangers-on who lounged outside the saloon.

"What're you lookin' at, you starin' idgit?" Goliath insolently demanded of the silent onlooker.

A primitive urge he'd never felt before told John to leap and throttle the man. He'd had but a single glance at the second man's contorted face but it had confirmed his worst suspicions. His father lay in the dusty street, struggling to rise but too drunk to do so. Supreme self-control held John back. He raised one eyebrow instead. "I always look when there's something to see."

It evidently disarmed the big man for he shrugged, grunted, and went back inside with seven-league strides.

The bored-looking crowd dispersed and John walked to his father. With arms of steel, he raised him, ignoring the other's protestations and wildly swinging arms. John also made sure to keep his face averted so he couldn't be seen. Even after all these years Dad might recognize him as the boy in a few pictures Grandfather had sent, now grown to manhood.

It took all his strength to hoist Talbot aboard Crowfoot, who chose to act skittish and received a blow just hard enough to convince him otherwise. Head up, lips set, he led the burdened horse out of town far enough so overly curious citizens could not hear what he meant to say. Beneath the shelter of a great Ponderosa pine he gently eased the crippled man to the needle-covered ground. He removed Crowfoot's saddle and propped his father against it, then with the wilderness skills he'd learned on his trek from New Mexico, made a small fire and brewed coffee. When Dad awakened from his stupor, he'd need it.

The waiting time felt endless. John swung between wishing he'd never come to knowing full well if he hadn't, all hope of Johnny Talbot ever being a real man again was nearly impossible. When the other stirred and groaned, his as-yet-unrecognized son whispered a prayer for help and guidance and poured coffee into his tin traveling cup.

"Who're you?" Still belligerent, Talbot glared but reached for the steaming coffee.

"I'm your son." He couldn't get anything else out.

The extended hand fell before it could take the cup. Fear leaped into the watching eyes. His face went dirty-white. "No!" He tensed, ready to spring, his gaze on John's face in awful fascination. "I'm dead, then, and you've come to torment me?"

Pity twisted like a knife in his son's middle. "No, Dad. I've come to help you and you aren't dead. Drink your coffee and I'll tell you everything."

His father's color slowly returned to normal but a haunted expression remained on his face. His hands shook so he could barely hold the cup. Yet by the time John told his simple story through three cups of the strong brew, a look not unlike the one his son had inherited had softened the haggard face. "You came."

"Yes. As soon as I knew and could." In the stillness of the pines the sound of a chipmunk scrabbling sounded loud.

"And you found me—like this."

John couldn't bear the forlorn misery in the words. He leaned forward, face intent. "Dad, the important thing is that we're together." He took a long breath. "There isn't anything that says you have to stay like this. You may be down but you're far from being out."

Black hatred dropped over Talbot's features like an ugly devil mask. His eyes glittered. "If it hadn't been for that skunk who called himself Smith, you'd have found me on the prettiest little spread in New Mexico," he ground out between clenched teeth. "Well, he's going to pay. I'll find him and when I do I'll rid Arizona of one of its crooked citizens." His hands clenched into fists.

John knew better than to argue, in spite of the terrible dread the threat brought. "Let's talk about it later. Right now, we need to find a place to stay." He thought for a moment. "Are you particularly fond of Flagstaff?"

His father snorted. "Fond! I don't care if I ever see it again." He finished the last of his coffee. "John, I'd give anything to settle the score with a certain saloon keeper before I leave."

"Good." His son laughed at the way Talbot's unshaven jaw dropped. "What do you think of this?" He outlined plans that brought remonstrations, then a gleeful grin before they began to carry them out. An hour later, a vastly different looking Johnny Talbot rode up to the

Frontier Saloon on a newly purchased black mare called
Lady. Both he and his companion wore outfits so spank-
ing new from boots to hats they fairly shouted for attention.

"All right, Dad. Remember, I'm John Ashley if anyone asks," he reminded. "Once they know who I really
am, we'll have trouble finding out what we want to know.
Do as we agreed, then we'll get out."

Johnny nodded, slid from the saddle, and marched into
the Frontier and up to the bar. John hesitated a moment,
then casually followed with a cluster of loiterers whose
murmurs, "Well, wouldja look at that" thrilled him to
the soul with the knowledge there was more than one
way to settle a score. He arrived inside just in time to
hear Goliath bellow.

"Thought I told you to—" He stopped. His eyes bulged.
"You—you—" A hint of foam sprang to his thick lips.

"I've come to pay off my debts. All of them." Johnny
Talbot's unflinching gaze never left the saloon keeper's
dumbfounded face. He pulled some of the bills John
had given him from his pocket, counted them out, and
demanded, "I want a receipt."

"Receipt!" A big hand snatched the money. "You
ain't sayin' you don't trust me, are you?"

The saloon grew deadly quiet but Talbot didn't budge.
"Give me a receipt."

"What's carrying on in here?" A burly man with a
silver star worn prominently on his leather vest elbowed
his way through the crowd and to the bar. "Talbot,
where'd you get those clothes?"

"A friend gave them to me." He didn't back down

and a strange pride and respect stole into his son's heart. "Sheriff, every man here will tell you I just paid off my debts in full. I asked for a receipt and he—" A pointing finger indicated Goliath. "He's trying to make something of it."

"That so?" Keen eyes shone beneath heavy brows. When the saloon keeper reluctantly nodded, the sheriff gruffly ordered, "Write him a receipt and mark it paid. In full." A hint of humor twitched his drooping mustache. "Glad you got yourself a friend, Johnny. If you and he are smart, you might want to locate elsewhere."

"We intend to." Talbot took the requested receipt laboriously written on a scrap of paper, pocketed it, and turned toward the door.

"You didn't say who your friend was," the sheriff called.

He turned an innocent face toward the lawman. His eyes opened wider. "Why, no, I didn't, did I?" In the stone-cold silence he walked to the door and out. Again John waited, this time wanting to applaud. So much the better for even his partial name not to be connected with Dad just now. He reveled in the dismay and shock that rippled through the room after several minutes went out. Lady and her rider had already disappeared. John mounted Crowfoot and turned him in the opposite direction, but once out of Flagstaff, he changed course and a little while later met his father on the western edge of town.

Johnny Talbot sat on his horse, a far cry from the miserable specimen who had groveled in the street such a short time before. His first sight of the son who had made it possible for him to again walk tall brought him from the saddle and laughter rang clean and good in the quiet spot. "I'll never forget it," he sputtered when he could again get control. "You were right. Confounding the enemy that way meant more than if I'd been able to pound him into the ground."

John's spirits leaped. Did he dare say what came to mind? Why not? "Dad, suppose you could play a similar trick on Dan Smith?" He saw his father stiffen and the laughter stilled.

"What do you mean?" Talbot crouched, hands extended, clenching and unclenching.

Necessity allowed for no wavering. "You have choices." He slipped from the saddle and faced his antagonist in what he knew would be one of the most crucial tests possible.

"Choices," John repeated. "When we find Smith, you can kill him and either hang or if you get a sympathetic jury, spend the rest of your life rotting behind bars." When his father flinched, he fiercely rejoiced. "For most of my life, you've been gone. Dad, is your hatred and desire for revenge more important to you than your only son? If you die or go to prison, you're deserting me the way you did when Mother died—and this time there will be no chance of getting you back."

Johnny Talbot grayed and staggered back. He tried twice to get his voice before he finally got out, "He cheated me. He took everything—and I built it up for you." Thwarted love rang through the heartfelt cry.

"What good is it, if we aren't together?" Back to the wall, John fought the age-old fight between good and evil, using every weapon he could muster. "Even if we never get a penny back, we have the farm back home or the money from it, if we choose to sell." The flame of righteousness filled him. "If we had nothing, how can satisfied vengeance compare when weighed against an eternity separated from each other—and from God?"

His father's body quivered. Great sweat drops sprang to his forehead. John knew long-forgotten or ignored truths learned at Grandfather and Grandmother's knees offered aid in the battle for a soul.

"What did you mean by confounding the enemy without killing him?" the tormented man hoarsely cried.

Bands of fear that had constricted John's chest loosened but he knew he had not yet won. "What if we find Dan Smith and not only recover what he stole but prove to all of Arizona Territory what kind of skunk has sneaked into its borders?" he flashed. The idea exploded. "You know him by sight, no matter what name he's using. He doesn't know me. The name John Ashley is meaningless to everyone here except us." Excitement fired him up. "Isn't he the kind of man who would rather be shot than shown up as a four-flusher?"

"Yes." Little by little Talbot relaxed and by the time they mounted and rode toward the setting sun, Johnny Talbot and his son had formed a partnership. A few days later they sat their horses above a small, run-down cabin John had purchased with some of the lease money. A few miles from Williams, it didn't look to be much but had great possibilities because of location, good grazing land, and two determined men. Johnny refused to make any of the trips into town for supplies and curtly added, "I can't say if I'm able yet to turn down a drink." His face twisted. "I know it's wrong but I just won't take the chance. There's too much at stake."

"I'm proud of you, Dad."

"I know." A look passed between them that lifted the younger man's spirits. He whistled all the way into town. Finding a certain needed wagon part wouldn't come in until the next day, he decided to stay over. Overheard praise of "the dandy grub at Harvey's Fray Marcos" encouraged him to try it out. He cleaned up, made his way to the restaurant, and with some difficulty chose his supper from the wide variety of items listed on the menu. He paid little heed to the girl who waited on him except to note her attractiveness, yet while he ate, he discovered his gaze returned to her busy self again and again. He compared her with a misty memory. Copper hair, hazel eyes, the right size. . . He started violently. Unless he'd taken leave of his wits, he'd found the girl he last saw shivering on a riverbank miles from Williams.

Now came a time of divided loyalties. John doggedly worked long hours on the place he'd bought but every time he got to town he tarried for a meal and when possible, chose the table serviced by the girl he'd learned to know as Miss Templeton, then Daisy, when a petite brunette addressed her one day. Too shy to identify himself, he admired from the distance of reserve. He noticed how she drew a fine line between courtesy and familiarity and secretly scowled when a tawny man someone called Winningham boldly stared at her.

The gold of autumn turned to dross. Sparkling winter billowed. John's frequent visits to town dwindled and he restlessly chafed at winter's confining hand but used the time well in planning with his father how they would buy a few cattle in the spring. Johnny had lost some of his hankering to keep moving on and confessed he liked the idea of settling down. They had long since decided to sell out in Illinois. "Too many painful memories there," he said.

Winter passed and so did the coldness in John's heart, the fear another man would capture Daisy Templeton's love before he even had the chance to get better acquainted. A new and separate gladness had also brought spring into his heart. Dad little resembled the pitiful creature he met in Flagstaff. Tall, strong, tanned, and eager, he'd begun listening when John read from Grandfather's Auld Book and one evening when swelling buds and pale green shoots promised resurrection he said, "I've sinned greatly. Is there forgiveness for me?"

"Yes, if you are willing to pay the price."

John saw the struggle that still raged in his father's soul before he whispered, "I'm trying" and his prayers for Johnny Talbot intensified until they became a constant cry to a merciful God.

John rode into Williams early one Sunday morning and attended church. A plain young preacher in a plain log church proclaimed the message of salvation to the gathered congregation. John felt he had truly come home. A glimpse of a bonnet with copper hair peeping out brought a smile and the next week, he talked his father into going with him. He noted with keen interest how Dad listened and nodded at certain places, the shine in his eyes when the minister read passages they had shared at home.

The service ended. They turned to go. John felt his father stiffen and followed his gaze to Rex Winningham, face half-turned from them. "It's him," Johnny hissed and his son's blood ran cold.

# eleven

John Talbot clutched his father's arm with an iron grip. "Don't do anything rash," he commanded in a voice designed to reach only his father's ear. For a heart-rending second he felt Johnny start to pull away, then an audible sigh followed and the brawny muscles relaxed. In unspoken agreement, they lingered until the tawny rancher went out, taking care to keep their backs toward Winningham in case he looked their way. By the time they reached the door, John glimpsed his father's enemy riding away on a fine horse.

"Whew, that was close," he muttered after greeting the preacher, nodding at other worshipers, and mounting Crowfoot while his father sprang to Lady's back.

"Too close." The black look John hated that hadn't appeared on the older man's face for some time fell like a heavy, smothering curtain. All signs of the softness inspired by the church service vanished before it and it took all the way home for the worried young man to put forth convincing arguments why they shouldn't immediately go to the marshall of Williams and demand justice. Johnny finally agreed showing their hand before having solid proof would gain nothing and the tension eased.

"I'm proud of you, Dad."

He didn't have to say why and the quick response, "I think I am, too," sent hope leaping. A few months earlier he'd have bitterly laughed had anyone suggested the self-control the persecuted man had shown today.

Now a sense of urgency returned. Winningham had obviously used his ill-gotten gains, along with other nefarious earnings, to buy his large holdings and establish himself as an important person in these parts. Once alerted to the possibility of losing them, the ruthless man would stamp out whoever stood in his way. The situation looked blacker than ever, yet night after night, John prayed, asking for things to be resolved and without bloodshed. His father didn't pray, at least aloud. Yet a certain stillness showed the magnificent fight going on inside him. He had long since conquered desire for whiskey, scorning it as unnecessary now that he had his son. If only he could also defeat hatred!

"The way I see it," he said one clear spring evening when a single star heralded the bouquet to follow in the Arizona skies. "Smith—Winningham must have records of his dealings. If we can get our hands on them. . ." His gleaming eyes and set face finished the sentence.

"I'm more concerned that he will find out who you are," John told him. He stared unseeingly at the quiet scene before him, one he had learned to love even more than his Illinois farm. "Dad, why don't you grow a beard and mustache? I know both of us have always hated them, but a disguise might prove invaluable." He listened to the *ooo-ooo* of a nearby owl, then added, "I might just be able to get papers, if there are any."

His father's strong frame jerked convulsively. "How?"

"I heard in town Winningham's making a large spring drive, selling off a bunch of cattle and horses. I hate a sneak thief, but it's your property, not his."

"I'd rather never get it back than lose you." Johnny Talbot gripped his son's hand. "I won't have you taking chances."

Heart singing, John promised caution—and threw it to the winds a week later. He had gone into Williams and again been held up for certain necessities. Dad wouldn't worry if he didn't come home. They'd discussed the need to reconnoiter and for John to learn as much of Winningham's movements as possible.

He stayed in the dining room as long as he could, watching Daisy Templeton and talking with her a bit, something he had begun with his first trip to town after winter snows no longer imprisoned him on the ranch. Any doubt that she was and would always be the only woman for him had melted with the white drifts. The magic of spring and new life surged through him, at times overshadowing his need to be watchful and alert.

Still, he couldn't help seeing how Rex Winningham's rude stare brought color then pallor to the Harvey Girl's sweet face. Tonight it happened again. The rancher said something in a low tone and received a glacial glare before Daisy marched away, head high, red streamers waving in her cheeks. It took a quick silent prayer to hold John in his seat and the look the catlike rancher exchanged with the men at his table made the onlooker wary. So did a muttered exchange of words not meant for his ears. He only heard snatches but enough to understand Winningham meant to waylay Daisy the next time she stepped out for a breath of fresh air, as she often did.

So the scoundrel had actually spied on her!  Red rage sprang full blown to John's brain but he forced it away. Anger accomplished far less than a cool head.  He rose, walked past the thieving rancher with a slight nod.  His keen hearing, sharpened by a feeling of impending action, had its own reward.  One of Winningham's cohorts mumbled, "Somethin' funny about that galoot. 'Tain't natcheral for a man not to talk more than he does."

"Two-bit homesteader trying to play rancher," his boss sneered.  John just grinned and kept on walking.  Someday, God willing, things would be a whole lot different. He stepped outside, make a show of walking to the livery stable and passing the time of day with the owner, then yawned, told the loquacious man goodnight, and strolled away.  Out of sight, he ducked into a side street and wended his way back to a safe position that offered an excellent view of the Fray Marcos, where he hunkered down for a wait.  With lightning calculations he figured just when Daisy would appear, if she did choose tonight to walk.  First, she'd finish her chores.  Next, change from her uniform into something softer; he'd seen her once or twice in a dainty gown with a shawl around her shoulders to ward of the cold night air.

"She can't be too late," he told himself.  "The way I hear it, if they break curfew they'll find the door locked." John grinned boyishly.  Stories ran rampant of rebellious Harvey Girls who refused to be so confined and broke curfew, then relied on persuading the night cook to let them in.  Others whose abodes had trees growing tall and close enough, sometimes climbed them and sneaked into obliging friends' unlocked windows. Special permission to be out past curfew meant lengthy explanations and excellent reasons to eagle-eyed housemothers.

Only twenty minutes remained before curfew when a slim, white-clad figure stepped outside the watched door. It hesitated, apparently scanning the deserted street, then stretched, lifted skirts with one hand, and stepped from the porch. At the same instant, John grew aware of a movement to his left. A large man came from behind the corner of the hotel and accosted the girl. John inched closer, unobserved and ready.

"May I walk with you, Daisy?" Winningham's unmistakable drawl sounded loud in the clear air and carried to the eavesdropper.

"Miss Templeton to you and I prefer to walk unaccompanied."

"Why not Miss O'Rourke?" Insolence underscored every word. John clenched his fists and silently stole closer, so close he hard Daisy gasp, too intent on the scene to comprehend its full meaning.

"What are you saying, sir?" If she were frightened, it didn't show in the way she challenged her tormentor and drew herself to full height. Enough twilight showed to light her upturned face.

"Think I'm a fool?" Winningham roughly jeered. "I make it my business to find out everything there is to know about those who—interest me." His mockery stopped just short of insult. "I have ways. Your employers will be mightly glad to learn the self-righteous, hymn-singing Miss Templeton isn't a Kansas lady at all but a —"

The first blow John Talbot had ever given another man felled him when it landed squarely on the point of his chin with all the young strength and fury gained by hard work and clean living. It effectively interrupted his revelations and the rancher fell without a cry.

"Don't be afraid, Miss Templeton. Go back inside." He gently took her arm and turned her toward the porch.

She stiffened. "Who are you?" But John didn't reply. If Winningham came to and recognized him, all his and Dad's plans would fail. He released her arm, courteously tipped his hat, and disappeared in the dusk that had crept over the street.

Shaken even more by the Western knight who had rescued her than by the realization she'd been found out, Daisy repeated, "Who *are* you?" Only a soft night wind answered, cooling her hot face and piercing her shawl until she felt cold inside. She stumbled back the way she'd come, praying she wouldn't encounter anyone. Luck held. She reached her room unobserved, burst inside, and locked the door behind her.

"Daisy, what's happened?" The book Noley had been reading fell to the richly carpeted floor and she sprang from her bed, black eyes concerned.

"I found him. I mean, he found me. Rex Winningham stopped me and—" To her utter disgust, she burst into angry tears that held a note of disappointment.

Noley just let her cry until the sobs ceased; Daisy blew her nose on the handkerchief her friend produced and scrubbed at her tear-stained face. "Now, what happened, for pity's sake?"

"I went out for a few minutes; the evening has been so

nice." Daisy dropped onto her bed and blew her nose again. "Rex Winningham got mad when I told him to call me Miss Templeton and that I didn't want his company. He asked why he shouldn't call me Miss O'Rourke."

"O-oh." A soft hand went to Noley's mouth. "How did he find out?"

"He said he had ways." Daisy shivered. "The bounder!"

"You should call him no-good polecat," the Southern girl put it, pansy eyes flaming with anger. "That's what the cowboys call bad men out here. Wait 'til I tell Mrs. Hill."

"You mustn't. And if he does, I'll be in terrible trouble." Daisy fought hard not to let tears come again.

"I don't see why," Noley reflected. "You are Daisy Templeton."

"But it sounds deceitful that I left off the O'Rourke, you have to admit that."

"Y-yes, but go on."

"He said my employers would be mighty glad to learn the self-righteous, hymn-singing Miss Templeton isn't a Kansas lady at all, but a. . ." She broke off just as Winningham had done, assaulted by a thought the way he'd been assaulted by an unknown defender. "Oh, no, he must have heard. What can he think? Winningham didn't finish his sentence."

Noley stared at her, bewilderment plain. "Are you crazy? How could he *not* have heard what he said?"

"I don't mean the rancher. I'm talking about the man who knocked him down in the middle of his accusations,"

Daisy explained. Her heart ached. "Oh, Noley, over-hearing just part of the story means my chivalrous hero will think I'm bad."

"He won't when you explain."

"I can't explain." Sheer misery straightened her spine. "When I asked him who he was after, he told me not to be afraid but he vanished so quickly I wondered if I'd dreamed him until I looked down and saw Winningham unconscious in the street." She drew in a long, quivering breath. "That's not all. Unless my ears are playing tricks, the man who intervened tonight is the same man who saved me at the train wreck."

Noley sat speechless, eyes like twin black stars.

"What if he's just passing through on the train? What if he's a cowboy who rides on tomorrow? As long as he lives, he will remember he leaped in to save someone unworthy of his noble act." Daisy had never felt worse and Noley's quick assurance that perhaps the man actually lived near Williams did little to lessen the pain in her heart. She simply couldn't bear having even a stranger think the worst of her, and that fatal interrupted sentence certainly left that impression. The possibility he and the hero of the earlier rescue were the same added agony. Yet the same spirit that led her father from Ireland, her mother to sail with the Mercer Brides, rose and gave courage.

"If Winningham comes in, ignore him," Noley advised. "I'll wait on him if I have to and if I'm reported, we'll tell Mrs. Hill the whole story."

Cheered by her friend's loyalty, Daisy managed break-fast, then dinner, then supper. To her great relief, the tawny rancher didn't appear. John Ashley, whose name she had finally learned, came in for supper and brightened her day. Although she had admitted it to no one so far, his quiet, mannerly way touched a wellspring of admiration in her. When winter kept him from coming, she'd missed him. With spring and his return, Daisy faced the truth: he meant far more to her than any man she'd ever known except her father, and the feelings she had about him in no way resembled her love for the merry Irishman.

A lull in business offered opportunity for a bit of conversation. John's dark brown gaze never wavered when he asked for more coffee then said, "Did you hear about the excitement?"

She nearly dropped the coffee urn. "Excitement?" Her hand trembled.

"Yes. The rancher Winningham left early this morning on one of the biggest cattle and horse drives ever held in this part of the territory."

"Why, how interesting," she faltered. Relief threatened to undo all the nerve she'd been clutching against having to see the obnoxious would-be swain.

John cut into the juicy roast beef. "Do you know him well? I notice he sits at your table."

"Well enough to wish he'd drive his cattle and horses and himself right on out of Arizona," she spiritedly told him, then bit her lip. "Mr. Ashley, forget I said that, please. We aren't supposed to have aversions. Or if we do, we aren't to show them."

"I'm a good secret keeper," he cryptically told her. For a heartbeat, the flicker of doubt crossed her mind but his next words reassured her. "Why, Miss Templeton, you'd be surprised at how well I keep my lip buttoned. I remember once. . ." He launched into a humorous story of the range and set her laughing. When he went out, a little smile still curved her lips and a warmth surrounded her heart. If what she saw in those dark eyes proved true, so might her long-held dream, and more and more she longed for love to come. In a few short months her contract would end. Mama and Daddy wouldn't want her to stay away longer—unless she had a husband.

Daisy turned tomato red and hastily began clearing away.

With the advent of nicer weather, the Harvey Girls widened their horizons by using carefully hoarded time off to see something of the country. Noley and Daisy eagerly boarded the train that took them the sixty miles north to the Grand Canyon. "If I weren't marrying Tom the day my contract ends, I'd love to work here," Noley confessed at first sight of El Tovar Hotel in all its splendor.

"So would I." Daisy gaped at the enormous, rambling structure. Privileged by their connections, they were shown the guest rooms: comfortable beds, spacious dressers; mirrors and rocking chairs—everything to make travelers comfortable. Hopi House, directly across from El Tovar, held native Indian arts and resembled the Hopi dwellings at Oraibi. The visitors stayed overnight and thrilled to the evening presentation of colorful dancers with their authentic Hopi songs and dances.

"I hope you don't come here," Noley whispered that night after they'd turned out the lights. "I love Tom but

you were my first friend. Daisy." She hesitated. "You
don't have much time left to find your cowboy." A yearn-
ing touched her words. "I've looked them over but the
only ones who have hung on when you refused to pay
attention are Rex Winningham—he's despicable—and
that nice John Ashley. He just has a little place, according to gossip. Would that make any difference, if you
loved him?"

Daisy smiled in the darkness. "No. Not if I loved him."
She treasured the thought and after long minutes decided
to confess how dear John had grown even with the small
amount of contact they'd had. "Noley?"

Only a soft, even breathing answered, showing how
well the day's walking to view the most wonderful sight
they'd ever seen also served as a powerful relaxant. Daisy
sighed, sorry yet half glad. This way she could hold
close feelings she scarcely admitted to herself, yet she
couldn't help praying, "Father, I'm so glad Noley thinks
John is nice. She's so wise about some things and I'm
so untried. Please, help me do Your will and be glad."
She fell asleep and dreamed of John .

๛

Sometime in the early morning hours, Daisy stirred and
awakened. She pinched herself to be sure she really lay
in a bed in the El Tovar Hotel of Arizona and that the
past months weren't all a long, exciting dream. She also
concentrated on two voices, one muffled through a bandana and smoke, the other low but familiar coming out
of the encroaching night. After a time, she nodded. They
were the same. She tried to think if she had ever heard
the voice elsewhere. A niggling feeling made her rest-

less, a wraith of memory that would solve her problem. If only she could remember! Yet like the veils of mist that swirled over the canyon, changing its appearance a hundred, nay, a million times a day, it eluded her. Another thought attacked her. Wonderful as John Ashley was, kind and dear and courteous, why did her mutinous heart yearn for her rescuer? What kind of woman was she, anyway, to compare a godly man—and she knew John was from his attitude in church and elsewhere—with a dancing shadow that had little substance? A shadow that stood for a stranger whose lips must curl with contempt at the irony of defending a girl without honor.

She writhed, twisting the sheets around her until a slight movement told her Noley had been disturbed. Daisy held her breath and forced herself to relax. Her friend stilled but Daisy's troubling thoughts did not. Until morning she simply marked time, knowing things always looked far worse in the deep dark. Morning and sunlight drove shadows away, at least until day died and night reigned again.

Once planted in her fertile brain, the struggle between her growing attachment for John Ashley and the insatiable desire to find and justify herself with her phantom hero interfered with concentration and enjoyment of the very land she'd longed to explore. It crept in unwanted at every opportunity. To worsen matters, John's visits to the dining room had completely ceased. Daisy looked and waited for him every day, telling herself that with spring work, of course he had less time to come riding in "like young Lochinvar" as Noley had once teased. Yet his absence strengthened her growing love, now mingled with fear. What if he had somehow heard of the disgraceful scene outside the hotel and felt her unwomanly? Even memories of the honest admiration in his frank face did little to console her.

❧

A week passed. Instead of feeling better, she felt worse all the time. One night she prayed, "Father, I've been so foolish, wanting my own way and clinging to childish dreams spun from improbable love stories. Forgive me and please, send John back." The hardest task she ever faced, even more so than leaping into a dark river, came when she forced herself to add, "If it be Thy will." Days limped by, into a second week. Rumor had it Winningham and his outfit were on their way back to Williams after a successful drive that resulted in riches just short of a gold mine.

"Just what I need," Daisy crossly told her mirrored reflection. "John disappears and RW owner returns bigger and braggier than ever. God, what am I going to do?"

When an answer came, she knew God had nothing to do with it. Surely Satan himself had inspired the note she received from Rex Winningham one afternoon just before time for her to start serving the evening meal. Decorously addressed to Miss Templeton, the envelope held a single sheet, a scrawled, unsigned demand.

*If you want to be known by your present name, Miss O'Rourke had better be all smiles and blushes at dinner and prepared to walk out with the best catch in Williams afterwards.*

# twelve

One by one the lights of the RW ranchhouse went out. A quiet darkness settled for the night.

One by one the stars went out, swallowed by rolling black clouds that boded well for John's mission. At dusk he had arrived at Rex Winningham's spread, tied Crowfoot a half-mile from the house, and wormed his way forward until he reached the frail shelter of low-growing bushes that greedily snatched at his clothing but offered the only hiding place he could see. From his vantagepoint, he watched a middle-aged woman who must be the housekeeper come to the porch, shake out a cloth, and later appear with a pan of dishwater, which she threw and barely missed him. Yet long after silence reigned supreme, John tarried. It wouldn't do to be caught at the job he hated but knew must be done.

A hundred times he and his father had discussed the risk and finally the older man consented. "Remember, if there's any kind of hitch, *get out*. Don't wait for anything."

Now the prowler shifted position, winced, and tore free from the prickly bush. Before he stepped to the porch, he removed his boots and carried them in his left hand. Praying desperately that the floor wouldn't creak, he softly stole across the porch and to the door, counting on the carelessness of Western folk who seldom locked up. The knob turned in his hand. He pushed the door open. His heart leaped. A few live embers in the fireplace cast a dim glow over the large room.

"Thanks, God," he whispered, wondering if such a prayer fit his doings. Step by step he crossed the room after his eyesight adjusted enough to discern a big, untidy desk on the side by the window. Once a floorboard gave and he held his breath but no one came. Again he moved forward until he reached the desk. Winningham was the kind of man to boast among his cronies about his dealings and keep records of them for his own satisfaction. John slid open a drawer, snatched a packet of papers, and held them up for inspection. The dying coals didn't offer light to read them. He cautiously set down his boots and struck a match, then quickly riffled through. Nothing suspicious there. He put them back, opened another drawer and repeated the performance but not until he drew forth papers from the bottom drawer did his spirits quicken. In bold, scrawled writing the names *Dan Smith* and *Johnny Talbot* leaped forth to condemn the rancher.

John hastily shoved the papers into his shirt front and carefully arranged others to hide their loss. In his jubilation he gave the desk drawer a harder push than necessary. The resulting screech sounded like a dull saw in green timber.

"Who's there?" a woman's voice demanded from a distant part of the ranchhouse.

John weighed possibilities. She had to enter the room the same way he had. The window was his best bet. Her grabbed his boots, slipped to it, and raised the sash as quietly as possible. He stepped through and gently closed it behind him. Still stocking-footed, he crossed the yard and melted into the shadows just before light flared in the room he had fled. The intruder threw himself flat on the ground and played possum, vowing never again to get involved in such a situation yet secretly rejoicing that proof of his father's claims lay warm and waiting inside his shirt.

After what felt like a lifetime, the ranchhouse again lay dark and John stole away. Aided by a belated moon that peered through the boiling clouds, he got to Crowfoot and mounted. Five minutes later, they were caught in a drenching rainstorm that hunkered John down in the saddle, soaked to the skin but wanting to yell. The downpour would erase any trace he or Crowfoot had left from their night marauding.

Uneasy daylight dawned when the weary pair reached home. Johnny Talbot waited in the open doorway. "Well?"

"I found papers but haven't had time to read them." John tossed the packet to his father, marched in toward the roaring fire in the fireplace, and exchanged wet clothing for a good rubdown and dry shirt and jeans.

"It's all here."

Something in the tone of voice whipped John around. "You don't sound as excited as I'd have imagined." He stared at the older man, struck by a strange look in his face that could only be described as peace.

Johnny's steady gaze met his son's unflinchingly. "All the time you were gone I though about a lot of things." He touched the papers he had laid on a table. "I felt this moment would be the highlight of my life, to be able to make up to you some of not being around while you grew up. Instead, I discovered nothing really matters except what you said when we first came here—that we be together through eternity. I asked God to forgive me and told Him if I could be a better man by not getting what was rightfully mine, it was square with me."

John knew he would remember the moment forever, the humbleness in his beloved father's face, the recognition of another Father's love. "That's great, Dad," he said huskily and held out his hand. The strong grip that followed said more than words.

In short order, they cooked breakfast, ate, and planned. Now that they had the evidence, what was the best way to use it? Johnny shrewdly observed, "Winningham's a big man around here. I'm not saying the sheriff in Williams is his tool but let's not take chances. If Winningham helped put him in office, the sheriff's more than likely to throw you in jail for trespassing and theft." He tapped the table with his fingers. "The rain's bound to have washed out any traces of your call." He grinned and looked little older than his son. "I suggest you saddle up and go find a U.S. Marshall, especially since this case crosses Arizona and New Mexico Territorial lines. You can casually inquire at Flagstaff where you might find a marshall. Don't even think of asking in Williams." Longing filled his eyes. "Wish I could go with you."

"Why not?" John stood and stretched. "We haven't yet bought cattle and we'll be riding Lady and Crowfoot." He yawned until his jaw felt it would break. "Give me a couple hours sleep and we'll head out."

"This ride's not much like the one heading west, is it?" Johnny said significantly, once they got underway.

John shook his head, thinking of the bitter, broken man who had ridden with him, crippled by hatred and hounded by drink. "Thank God it's not" They lapsed into silence broken only by the steady drum of hoofbeats. "We could have taken the train, you know."

"I like the fresh air. Besides, the lawman we need may not be conveniently waiting for us alongside the track."

❧

His dry comment turned out to be prophetic. It took time to track down the closest U. S. Marshall and present their case, in a town so small it hardly seemed worthy to be called one.

"Marshall," John told the lanky man with gimlet eyes used to ferreting out truth. "From what I could see of some of the other papers, it appears Winningham's actually the head of the syndicate who makes it their business to force small ranchers out so they can gobble up the range around El Cinco.

"May I be so bold as to ask just how you happened to see such evidence?" the marshal sarcastically asked. "Breakin', enterin', and walkin' off with other men's property's a crime, mister. Why shouldn't I run you in?"

"Is walking into an unlocked house and taking what belongs to you a crime?" John's dark brown gaze never wavered.

A withered grin lit the lean face. "Reckon not." He reflected for a minute. "When's this Smith or Winningham or whoever he is due back from his cattle drive?"

"Soon."

The succinct answer brought the marshall to his feet. "Then what're we waitin' for? We'll ride to the nearest stage stop. I'll head for Williams and do some pokin' around."

"Should we come with you?"

"Naw. Just get yourself back soon as you can. I'll lay low 'til you get there." His eyes gleamed and anticipation filled his voice. "I reckon we'll throw this little s'prise party soon as the guest of honor comes in off the drive."

"He won't give in without a fight," John warned. "If you accuse him on his place, Winningham will start a ruckus and if the men I've seen with him represent the caliber of his outfit, there'll be blood spilled."

The marshal shot him a keen glance. "An' you don't want that."

"No," Johnny Talbot put it. "We just want what's ours."

A diabolical idea crept into John's mind. "There's another way." He could feel a smile begin in his heart and spread over his face. Glee filled him. "Winningham rides into town and has supper at the Fray Marcos a lot of nights, usually with just one or two of his riders."

"That's a Harvey place, ain't it?"

John nodded.

The marshal pursued the thought. "An' it ain't so likely our man will kick up a fuss in front of a lot of witnesses who won't lie for him. Son, you're plumb intelligent. Now, where's your spread? After I get what I need at the RW, why, I'll just mosey over to your place and wait for you. We'll also wait 'til the big drive's over. Then we'll have him." A strong hand closed tight in a gesture of triumph.

Days later, the marshal rode out from Williams one morning and told the Talbots, who had gotten home a short time earlier, "Saddle up. Word in town is that the RW outfit's gettin' in today and aimin' to paint the town. We'll be there."

❧

At the same time nemesis in the form of a U. S. Marshal and the Talbots quietly rode into town from different directions, having taken the precaution to separate outside it borders, Daisy O'Rourke's shaking hands clutched her enemy's threatening note. How could she overcome her fear and revulsion enough to pacify Winningham? What if she did walk out with him afterwards? Doing so meant risking insult. Refusing surely would bring anything from a sharp reprimand to dismissal.

The letter fell to the carpet. Daisy knelt by her bed, heedless of rumpling her starched skirt and spotless apron. "God, You are the only One Who can help me. Please. I need You so much." Only a few minutes remained for her to quickly bathe her face yet an inner peace swelled. So did the memory of a favorite Bible verse. Philippians 4:13, "I can do all things through Christ which strengtheneth me." She hugged it to her heart and threw her shoulders back, then before she could change her mind, ran lightly downstairs, head high and sustained by the promise.

A quick survey of the large room with its sparking

crystal, well-polished silver, and snowy tablecloths showed a lack of diners. She finished last-minute arrangements and stood waiting for her fiery trial, not knowing what she'd do but aware of a strength beyond her own.

Rex Winningham entered, slicked up as though he were getting married, Daisy contemptuously thought. Under cover of being seated along with two of his men, the tawny rancher whispered, "Well? Which is it?"

Daisy paused, again frantically praying for help. It came unexpectedly. From the corner of her eye she noticed John Ashley and Johnny Talbot enter the room, accompanied by a lanky stranger. She turned her head and smiled. John's face lighted and his dark brown eyes glowed, giving the tormented young woman the extra spark of courage to choose her course.

"Will you order now, Mr. Winningham? I'm afraid I don't have much time for you. Others are waiting," she said clearly.

The way he shoved back his chair and leaped to his feet showed he had read the hidden meaning in her reply. His action pulled the white cloth awry and sent china, silver, and crystal crashing to the floor.

"What seems to be the trouble here?" a freezing voice demanded. Mrs. Hill, in full sail, bore down on them. "Mr. Winningham, I'm afraid we'll have to ask you to leave. This is the second time you have transgressed the rules of our establishment."

"Leave?" he sneered. "I won't be the one thrown out when I tell you what I know about one of your waitresses." A cougar at bay, he prepared to stand his ground, claw, and rend.

"Sorry, Mr. Smith, but before you go shootin' off your mouth we'd like to hear how many folks you swindled out of their ranches," a drawling voice said from behind him.

Winningham whirled. "Who're you and why'd you call me Smith?" His insolent gaze swept from the tall man who produced a silver badge past John Ashley to the third man. His eyes bulged. His face turned livid. "Johnny Talbot?" His mouth hung open.

"The same, Dan Smith. The man you sold a ranch you didn't own near El Cinco."

Although Daisy didn't understand anything happening, she knew she'd been reprieved.

"I've never been in New Mexico Territory," Winningham shouted.

"Then how do you know where El Cinco is?" John Ashley smiled a curious smile, one so unlike the one he'd given Daisy that she started. "And how do you know my father?"

"Father! Say, what in blazes is the meaning of this?" the rancher blustered but a hunted look came into his eyes.

A ripple of shock ran through the now-filled room. Even Mrs. Hill forgot to protest but stood transfixed by the scene.

The lanky man took control. "Now, Mr. Winningham-Smith, we have solid proof of your crooked dealin's. Let's not keep these good folks from enjoyin' their supper any longer." In a lightning quick move a pistol sprang to his rock-hard hand. "Just tell your men to go on out, slow and easy. Then you and me will take us a little trip to the sheriff's office. You're goin' to have a lot of time to spend thinkin' about what you've done. You'll have comp'ny. The Territorial Prison at Yuma's got a lot of rattlesnakes." Still talking, he herded his prisoner out and called from the doorway, "Sorry, folks," then vanished with a thoroughly cowed Winningham.

Like stone figures brought to life, diners found their tongues and wagged them. Mrs. Hill ordered, "Don't just stand there, girls. Serve." The stern discipline and her commanding presence restored a semblance of order. Noley sent a commiserating glance at Daisy when their paths crossed but neither had time to discuss the unheard-of events. Nor did Daisy get to speak with John, who had announced himself as John Talbot's son. She had no time to do more than briefly speculate the difference in names and when her shift ended, Mrs. Hill beckoned her to follow to a small, deserted room.

"Now, Miss Templeton. Do you care to tell me exactly why this—person has been hounding you and what it it he seems to know that I don't?" Not an iota of the motherly woman's usual kindness showed.

Daisy's spirits dropped to the soles of her feet. "That's just it, Mrs. Hill. I'm not just Miss Templeton, I'm Daisy Templeton O'Rourke."

"I find nothing reprehensible about that," the amazing woman started. "Except that for some reason you're ashamed of your surname. My dear, are your parents such that you cannot honorably bear their name?"

"My parents are the finest, dearest, best Christians who ever lived," she cried. "Mrs. Hill, it's I who am dishonorable." In vivid sentences she sketched her background, her longing to see the southwest and the impossibility of it happening. "My cousin Daphne helped me learn to be lady-like so I could be a Harvey Girl," she finished breathlessly. "But Daisy O'Rourke sounds stagey and half the people I met in Kansas thought we still have Indian uprisings in Washington State so I just left off my last name and said I came from Kansas. I did—just not originally."

Mrs. Hill's stern countenance collapsed into laughter. "Young lady, if the worst thing you ever do is to travel under just part of your name, you needn't fear the consequences."

The temptation to admit to a lot more former conduct lapses died a-borning. "You mean I won't be dismissed?"

"No. I do suggest that as long as so little time remains in your contact you simply continue to be known as Daisy Templeton to avoid confusion and gossip." Mrs. Hill bent a knowing look at the culprit. "I wouldn't be at all surprised if the matter of the name wouldn't be resolved quite satisfactorily in the near future. Now, get to bed, child. You've had a long day."

Daisy held in the giggles until she reached her room and Noley. Then relief exploded and she repeated the conversation verbatim. "I don't understand what she meant about the name," she ended.

Noley's silky eyebrows shot up. Her black-pansy eyes sparkled. "Mrs. Hill is a wise woman who knows a lot more about what's going on with her girls than anyone believes," she said. "I've seen her watch John Ashley watching you." She smirked. "Once it's Daisy Ashley, you won't have to worry about either Templeton or O'Rourke, now will you?"

"For mercy's sake, go to sleep!" Daisy fired a pillow, dodged when it came back, and lay awake half the night reliving the evening. The exhilaration of no longer traveling under an alias died when she remembered John knew nothing of why Winningham—if that were really his name—threatened to expose her. She both longed for and dreaded the final showdown that must come. The next morning following her breakfast chores when the man who occupied such a prominent place in her dreams approached her, Daisy's traitorous heart pounded beneath her demure white bib.

"May I speak with you, please?" he asked. Big hat in hand, dark eyes shining, still a shy look made him resemble a small boy asking for another cookie.

"Of course."

Mrs. Hill stepped up with an alacrity that suggested wide open ears. "If you care to use the small room where we met last night, that will be acceptable," she told Daisy. "Just leave the door ajar, please." She swept away from a scarlet-faced young woman who meekly led her interviewer to the designated room.

Inside and seated, John began. "May I tell you a story?"

"Why, yes." Daisy found herself caught up in the tale of a motherless and then fatherless boy, of a young man who lost Grandmother and Grandfather then came West to find them.

She clenched her hands at the way Winningham had cheated Johnny Talbot and her hazel eyes opened wider when John gravely said, "I realized the name John

Talbot would hinder my search to restore Dad's losses so I traveled under my real first and middle name. Daisy—" She had a feeling he didn't even realize he had called her that. "I left my horse Crowfoot in Holbrook because a sense of urgency not to be denied filled me. At the time I believe God sent it on my father's behalf. I found out differently in the midst of smoke and fire."

She turned rigid. "Then, it was *you*. All the time." Why hadn't she known? Her heart felt harrowed. "You. In the overturned coach and the dark river." She shivered uncontrollably. "I never even got to say thank you!"

"A knock on the head and a delayed reaction landed me back in Holbrook," he explained. "But when I rode on, the memory of the girl God had permitted me to save never left." He squared his shoulders. "I knew from your voice the night I knocked Winningham out you recognized me. Not as John Ashley but as the stranger who rode a train knowing there was a reason." He reached strong hands out and took hers, hands that had once torn wreckage from her legs and body to free her. Now she felt free again, but chilled when he continued.

"I don't know what Winningham started to say that night. I do know you're the finest, most wonderful woman I have ever known. You're the only one I've ever loved, as well. Daisy, haven't you seen how it is with me each time you served me? I'm not good at hiding my feelings."

"You have that much faith in me?" she cried. Never had she felt so humble. To think that all along God had planned for her to receive a love akin to His own—beautiful in its selflessness. "John Ashley—the only thing Winningham knew was that I'm really Daisy Templeton O'Rourke, not a fine Kansas lady, but a Washington State mill owner's daughter."

"Thank God! I feared a 'fine Kansas lady' would never even consider an Illinois farm boy turned Arizona rancher. Would a certain Washington mill owner's daughter think about learning to love me and marrying me the day her contract ends?"

Daisy threw restraint to the corners of the room and herself into John's arms. "She already does love you, more than life itself, and she'll marry you the day *after* her contract ends; if Noley and Tom agree, we'll have a double ceremony."

A long sweet time later when Mrs. Hill coughed suggestively and opened the door a little wider before going on down the hall, John kissed his fiancee tenderly. "How could any man be more blessed? Daisy in his home and daisies blooming around his ranchhouse door."

Lost in the dream he painted, she wondered how she ever could have longed to be called otherwise. Guinever, Yolanda, even Marissa couldn't compare with Daisy, flower of the West, when John spoke her name in reverence and in love.

## Coming Soon. . .
## Flower of the North

A poignant story of a man who must rebuild
his life in the frozen wastes of Alaska in the
1890s. This exciting novel introduces new
characters and a courageous heroine to whom
dog sled travel and blizzards are more familiar than sky and tundra.

# *A Letter To Our Readers*

Dear Reader:

In order that we might better contribute to your reading enjoyment, we would appreciate your taking a few minutes to respond to the following questions. When completed, please return to the following:

Rebecca Germany, Editor
Heartsong Presents
P.O. Box 719
Uhrichsville, Ohio 44683

1. Did you enjoy reading *Flower of the West*?
   ❑ Very much. I would like to see more books
      by this author!
   ❑ Moderately
      I would have enjoyed it more if _____

   _____

2. Are you a member of **Heartsong Presents**? ❑Yes ❑No
   If no, where did you purchase this book? _____

   _____

3. What influenced your decision to purchase this
   book? (Check those that apply.)

        ❑ Cover        ❑ Back cover copy

        ❑ Title          ❑ Friends

        ❑ Publicity    ❑ Other_____

4. How would you rate, on a scale from 1 (poor) to 5
   (superior), **Heartsong Presents'** new cover design?_____

5. On a scale from 1 (poor) to 10 (superior), please rate the following elements.

___Heroine    ___Plot

___Hero    ___Inspirational theme

___Setting    ___Secondary characters

6. What settings would you like to see covered in **Heartsong Presents** books?_____

_____

_____

7. What are some inspirational themes you would like to see treated in future books?_____

_____

_____

8. Would you be interested in reading other **Heartsong Presents** titles? ❏ Yes    ❏ No

9. Please check your age range:
   ❏ Under 18    ❏ 18-24    ❏ 25-34
   ❏ 35-45    ❏ 46-55    ❏ Over 55

10. How many hours per week do you read? _____

Name _____

Occupation _____

Address _____

City_____ State_____ Zip _____

# Heart♥ng

## HISTORICAL ROMANCE IS CHEAPER BY THE DOZEN!

*Any 12 Heartsong Presents titles for only $26.95 ***

Buy any assortment of twelve *Heartsong Presents* titles and save 25% off of the already discounted price of $2.95 each!

**plus $1.00 shipping and handling per order and sales tax where applicable.

### *HEARTSONG PRESENTS TITLES AVAILABLE NOW:*

# Presents

## Great Inspirational Romance at a Great Price!

**Heartsong Presents** books are inspirational romances in contemporary and historical settings, designed to give you an enjoyable, spirit-lifting reading experience. You can choose from 144 wonderfully written titles from some of today's best authors like Colleen L. Reece,

*When ordering quantities less than twelve, above titles are $2.95 each.*

# Hearts♥ng Presents
## *Love Stories Are Rated G!*

That's for godly, gratifying, and of course, great! If you love a thrilling love story, but don't appreciate the sordidness of popular paperback romances, **Heartsong Presents** is for you. In fact, **Heartsong Presents** is the *only inspirational romance book club*, the only one featuring love stories where Christian faith is the primary ingredient in a marriage relationship.

Sign up today to receive your first set of four, never before published Christian romances. Send no money now; you will receive a bill with the first shipment. You may cancel at any time without obligation, and if you aren't completely satisfied with any selection, you may return the books for an immediate refund!

Imagine. . .four new romances every four weeks—two historical, two contemporary—with men and women like you who long to meet the one God has chosen as the love of their lives. . .all for the low price of $9.97 postpaid.

*To join, simply complete the coupon below and mail to the address provided.* **Heartsong Presents** romances are rated G for another reason: They'll arrive *Godspeed!*

---